YAH'S WAY

The Original Self-Help Culture

By

Solomon H. Johnson

Acknowledgement

First, I would like to thank the creative forces, YHWH, for allowing me the privilege and honor to receive the Spirit of Diligent Study and Open Channels of Frequency.

I would like to thank my parents for introducing me to the truth at the early stages of life. Diane Johnson, my mother, and my father, Jeff. I would also like to thank the brothers Yahshua Ross, Jerimyah Johnson, Yoseph Evans, Yaharam Yisrael, Baruk, Amaziah, Mikael, Victor Hezekiah Mason, Brother Shelomoh, Marquos, Azriel, Ya'aqob, and all who aided me in the painstaking study and relentless search for the Truth. Thank you!

To all scholars and elders who came before me in an effort to enlighten the children of Israel about who they are.

Ben Ammi, R.I.P., Obidyah Israel and Ysraylite Heritage, and those who are part of that organization, Elder Moses Farar, Ella J. Hugley, Nabi Melchizedek Y. Lewis, F. S. Cherry, Prophet William S. Crowdy, and all the writers of literature whose books I have read and studied over the years. Thank you.

The truth shall set you free!

INTRODUCTION

In recent times, there has been a surge in self-help idealism around the globe, with authors such as Rhonda Byrne, Joseph Murphy, Charles Hannel, and others who very seldom quote from ancient scripture. Perhaps this is for marketing purposes, yet they do occasionally reference scripture. This book is intended to show the reader the source of all self-help books, tracing them to the most ancient origins, and to explain why the Hebrew script is the most important writing in the world, both in past and present times.

I want to show how important the original language of the Hebrews is in attesting to the fact that the Bible itself is a self-help book. Most people will agree with the statement above, saying to themselves, "Sure, everyone knows that." However, it is much more profound than simply recognizing Proverbs, Ecclesiastes, and Psalms. In fact, the very name of the Hebrew Deity, YHWH, means "The Self-Existing Power," and nearly every story and historical record within the pages of the Hebrew Scriptures details the reliance upon the power that exists within one's self. This understanding is only reached when we accept the true meaning of our Creator's name. Only then can we begin to fathom the importance of the name of the Hebrew Israelite Deity.

You shall not misuse the name (laws) of YHWH, your very Power, for YHWH will not leave unpunished anyone who takes His name in vain. (Exodus 20:7)

Throughout the course of this book, we will find that the replacement names of the Hebrew Deity are exposed as frauds and tools meant to divert readers of Scripture from receiving the message originally given by the ancient scribes. Examples within the pages of Scripture attest to the fact that it was the power of self, the laws of attraction, and the subconscious mind that freed the Hebrews from the bondage of Egypt and was used to perform miracles throughout the history of the Israelites.

Self-help authors have produced literature with the intent to help others achieve what they want out of life, while I myself have focused on health, wisdom, positivity, and the welfare of all people. However, when reading most self-help books, there is almost always a principle of finance involved. The focus tends to be on how to get rich. Though the mind is elaborated upon and its inner workings revealed, the dominant focus is still on how to make more money. Mind you, the new generation of authors have great intentions, yet they have lost sight of the bigger picture.

Just as these very mind books teach us, the mind takes on the attributes of our dominant thoughts. As a result, money outweighs nearly everything else presented. And yes, we can benefit financially, but at what cost? If we are not careful, someone else may suffer as a result of our gain.

From Mount Halak, which rises toward Seir, to Baal Gad in the valley of Lebanon at the foot of Mount Hermon, he captured all the kings and put them to death. (Joshua 11:17)

No one can be the slave of two masters. He will either hate the first and love the second, or be attached to the first and despise the second. You cannot be the slave of both YHWH and money. (Matthew 6:24)

In hurting others, we hurt ourselves, for we are all connected in the universal mind and the physical one-world community. Readers of self-help books are often awed by the insight found in such literature, which gives detailed explanations of the inner workings of the creative process. However, the power of thought and the manifestation of one's desires often lure unsuspecting people into acquiring this knowledge for their own benefit. With the focus on riches and the prosperity of their own self-progression, they neglect the rest of the world community to which they belong.

For every action, there is a reaction; for every reaction, there is another, and it continues on as a never-ending sequence of events. Our minds must be focused on equality for all people in regard to health, academics, social behavior, and finance as well. Imagine owning your own home, the largest in your town, with storehouses of food and endless supplies, while the rest of your neighbors are poor and without the necessary means to survive a coming drought or famine. The poor may develop thoughts about how to acquire what you have, whether through positive means or negative actions, which could cause a rift between classes. Ultimately, this could lead to violence, theft, and even war accompanying the famine. However, if everyone were on one accord educationally, socially, and financially, then a foundation for the camaraderie and survival of the entire community would be in place.

The example above is the reason why the Essene community, to which the New Testament Messiah belonged, required its inhabitants to turn over their belongings to the leaders of the community, who would then redistribute them evenly among all. This practice of sharing eliminated jealousy, envy, hatred, and insecurity regarding the financial status of others. The wealth of the Essene sect was based on health, love, family, and respect for one another. In this author's opinion, the writers of self-help books ought not to encourage individual prosperity but should instead promote safety, well-being, health, and positive social behavior for all humankind.

In *Anacalypses Vol. 2* by Godfrey S. Higgins, the famed historian explores the history of the origin of language and concludes that communication in some ancient civilizations began with symbolism and evolved into organized spoken language. The language of the trees was universal and understood by all the earth's inhabitants, as evidenced by the written script of the Asian people of the East. Though the spoken languages may differ among Asians of various regions, the Mandarin letter characters carry the same meanings across much of Asia, providing an effective means of communication. The script, for the most part, reflects the overall nature of Egyptian hieroglyphs.

The Hebrew language, or rather its writings, were surely designed to be the most dominant language on Earth, and arguably still are, considering the heavy presence of Hebrew in nearly every language around the world. Hebrew, the language of the angels, was passed on to the human family, who used it to call upon the angels for assistance in earthly affairs.

All who call upon the name of YHWH will be saved. (Yoel 3:5)

This brings us to the name of the Israelite Deity, YHWH, who, according to the Hebrew Scriptures, is the Creator of all things, including the angels. But what exactly does YHWH mean? For the answer, we must consult the language and culture of the Hebrew people. The word YHWH represents passive creation, productivity, or birth. Together they form *Yah* (Force) and *Hawah* (Reception and Revolution); hence the name YHWH, which is simplified in meaning as "the power that exists of itself," or "the Self-Existing Power."

It has no beginning and no end. No one knows where it comes from, and no one knows where it is going. Native American tribes such as the Lakota call it the Great Life Mystery. Hebrews call it *Ahayah Asher Ahayah*, "the will that wills to be all that is." Therefore, the true definition of the Hebrew Israelite Deity is that which cannot be defined in terms of origin or reason. We, as human beings, are blessed to know only in part how it works. Its origin, destination, reason, and purpose are all unknown and undefined. What we do know, as conscious humans, is that this power exists within all things and that we are blessed with free will to use the energy that it is. The Hebrew writings teach us how to use and harness this energy for the greater good of all creation.

Peace on Earth is based upon obedience to what is natural. And yes, death is part of what is natural. However, mankind was created with the mind of reason and free will. Humanity has the opportunity to obtain states of consciousness unattainable by the average created being. For thousands of years, the question of the meaning of life has been posed with no certain answer. Are we to go through all the trials and tribulations of life and then die? Absolutely not. If that were the case, the life of man would be meaningless.

When consulting the oldest known epics concerning the creation of man, we see that man was made to maintain the Garden, which is the existence of existence itself. A garden is a place where things are grown and nurtured. (See: Ancient Sumerian Cuneiform Creation Epic, also *Bareshith* chapters 1, 2, and 3 in the Hebrew writings.)

ETYMOLOGY

The study of the origin of words is extremely important in finding and understanding truth. Below is a list of words used as substitutes for the source of all things that exist, accompanied by short definitions of their ancient origins to help give a proper understanding of these terms.

1. **Ba'al** – A word of ancient origin that derives from the Aryan root *baal*, which means "to shine." It was used as the name of a Canaanite deity and is also identified with the ancient Babylonian Sun God. It is further associated with Zeus and Jupiter. Whether by accident or intent, this word *Baal* was translated from the ancient Hebrew Shemitic word to the English word "Lord."

2. **Gad/God** – An ancient Hebrew/Shemitic word used by the astrologers of Babel as an alternate name for Jupiter (Zeus). This deity was also known among the Canaanites as *Ba'al Gad*, or "The Lord of Fortune." The name is also found among the Germanic peoples as *Goda* or *Gud*. In Isaiah 65:11, it is used as a proper name referring to the deity of fortune, showing the distinction between YHWH and Gad. The word also has roots in the European term referring to a union of the sexes, though "fortune" is the most common meaning. Jacob's son was named Gad on account of Leah, who felt fortunate to have borne a child for her husband through her handmaid Zilpah.

3. **Allah – El – Elah – Elohim** – Meaning "Mighty One," "High One," or "Most High." These are very ancient words used among the Hebrews as titles rather than proper names. They refer to the position of YHWH as ruler and creator of all things. These are titles, not explanations of the nature or duties of the Creator.

4. **Jesus – Iesous** – According to the *Greek to English Lexicon* by Liddell and Scott, this word is associated with the Greek goddess of healing, as well as with the god Zeus and the Egyptian goddess Isis.

5. **Adoni** – Means "Lord of the land," "Master," or "Landlord."

6. **Hashem** – Literally means "The Name" in Hebrew and is used as a replacement for the name YHWH by modern Jewish converts, who claim that the name YHWH is too holy to utter or pronounce. This practice goes against the Scriptures themselves. (See *Holy Bible*, Genesis 12:6–8; Exodus 20.)

7. **Jehovah** – The vowel points of the modernized Hebrew alphabet were combined with the Tetragrammaton YHWH and the word *Adoni*. Additionally, the letter "J" was added, though there is no equivalent sound in Latin, Greek, or Hebrew. As a result, the pronunciation of the name "Jehovah" came into existence.

TRUTH OF DEFINITIONS

The study of the origin of words is extremely important in finding and understanding truth. Below is a list of words used in Scripture with the intent to confuse the reader. Hebrew words can have several definitions which are determined by the context of usage. A few key words have been intentionally translated with the purpose of misinforming the seekers of truth. Below is a short list of words, their definitions, and examples of how they are used erroneously.

1. **Heart:** Equivalent to the Hebrew word *Leb.* In Hebrew, the definition of *Leb* (Heart), according to the Strong's Concordance, is: Center of, Care for, to Consent, Considered, Midst, Courageous, Friend, Kindly, Mind, Understanding, Wisdom.

In the typical English translation of the Hebrew Scriptures, when the word *heart* is replaced with *mind*, *thoughts*, or *wisdom*, the passages become clear where there was confusion before. See the examples below.

- **Exodus 28:30** – "And they shall be upon Aaron's heart" should read as "And they shall be upon Aaron's mind or thoughts."

- **Exodus 9:35** – "The heart of Pharaoh was hardened" should read as "The mind of Pharaoh was made up."

- **Genesis 27:41** – "And Esau said in his heart" should read as "And Esau thought to himself."

- **Jeremiah 7:24** – "The imagination of their evil heart" should read as "The imagination of their evil minds," for people imagine with their minds, not their emotions.

- **Isaiah 44:19** – "And none considereth in his heart" should read as "And none considereth in his thoughts."

- **Ecclesiastes 8:16** – "I applied mine heart to wisdom" should read as "I applied my mind to wisdom."

We as humans apply, consider, imagine, and speak first with our minds. Therefore, in nearly every instance where the word *heart* is used in English translation, it should read or be replaced with *mind* or *thoughts*. Why, then, does the Hebrew word *Leb* come to be translated as *heart* instead of *mind*? Doesn't it make more sense to translate *Leb* as *mind* based on the above examples?

2. **Fear:** In Hebrew, the word is pronounced *Yare* or *Yirah*. The definition of the word *fear* according to Strong's Concordance is: Afraid, Reverence. According to Webster's Dictionary, the word *reverence* is defined as: Revere, to show respect to, "reverence," or to worship and adore; a gesture of respect (as a bow or curtsy), respect shown or felt.

We see by the Hebrew definition of *fear* that it has opposite meanings depending on the context in which it is used. In Scripture translations, the word *fear* is often used in regard to the worship of YHWH. *"But you shall fear YHWH" (Leviticus 25:17).*

In my personal opinion, the average understanding of the word *fear* as it relates to the Western mindset is something dreadful. So why would anyone want to interact with something they fear? I would rather interact with something I love.

If I fear heights, large bodies of water, tigers, lions, or bears, I would certainly not want to engage with either situation. I would stay away from the things, I fear. However, if I adore, worship, honor, or am devoted to something, I would draw closer. Therefore, wouldn't it be more sensible to translate the word *Yare* as *reverence* instead of *fear*?

Now that we have an understanding of the proper translation, let us look at a few examples:

- **Deuteronomy 6:13** – "Thou shalt fear YHWH your power" should read as "Thou shalt adore YHWH your power."

- **Deuteronomy 10:12** – "But to fear YHWH thy mighty power, to walk in all His ways, to love Him, to serve Him" should read as "But to worship YHWH your mighty power, to walk in all His ways."

The examples below show how *Yare* is translated as *fear* or *afraid* according to its proper context in Strong's Concordance:

- **Genesis 46:3** – "Fear not to go down to Egypt."

- **Deuteronomy 28:66** – "And thou shalt fear day and night."

Based on the correct translations of Genesis and Deuteronomy, we see the importance of context and how the translators of the English versions either mistakenly or deliberately failed to use caution in understanding the contextual nature of certain words.

When you think of the island of Jamaica, you automatically think of Black people with distinct accents and dreadlocks, tropical weather, and so on. As with many things, our minds relate things to what we know them as. The same goes for Scripture. The word *Yare*, whose definition varies, is most often translated as *fear*, as in *afraid*, in regard to the worship of our Creator.

As a result, our minds, both consciously and subconsciously, are saturated with the idea that we should be afraid of YHWH. Consequently, we consciously and subconsciously avoid what we fear, and that thought manifests itself into the physical world, causing us to fear, avoid, and even dislike YHWH our Power as a result of repetitive erroneous translations. YHWH is now associated with *fear.*

Shatan has launched a full-scale attack on our minds, and we must become aware if we wish to fight back.

3. **YHWH** – Erroneously translated as *God* or *Lord.* The definition of YHWH is "The Self-Existing Power of creation" or "The Power that wills all things to be."

With the understanding of the name YHWH as the Power that exists of itself and within one's self, we can now properly understand what YHWH was saying to Moses in Exodus 3:13–15.

Exodus 3:15 – "This is what you shall say to the children of Israel, 'YHWH, the Alahim of your fathers...'" should read as "This is what you are to say to the children of Israel: The Power that exists within yourselves has sent me to you."

4. **Ahayah** – Correctly translated as "I AM" or "I AM THAT WHICH I AM," is found in Exodus 3:14. So YHWH said to Moses: "I will be what I will to be... The will to be has sent me."

Now that we have a better understanding of the situation, we can see that Exodus 3:7–15 explains how the cries (prayers) of the children of Israel were heard and seen by the creative forces that embody the will to be. As a result, YHWH allowed a savior to be manifested in the person of the prophet Moses, who was sent to the Israelites to free them from bondage.

Yes, a request was made first in Exodus 3:7, and then YHWH, the universal power of mind as one with the mind of man, heard and answered the prayers of the people of Israel.

Who is God? What is God?

Billions of people around the world ask themselves these questions with no satisfactory answer given. "The Man Upstairs," "A Higher Power," "The Great Architect," "Most High," and others are common expressions. Many attempt to explain God or the nature of God, yet none of these titles can truly express the truth behind the nature of the creative power.

Before the Hebrew prophet Abraham fathered the monotheistic belief system and understanding, the ancient cultures worshipped many substitutes. In the days of Noah, before and after the flood, Earth's inhabitants worshipped the beings that descended from the skies in fiery clouds.

Then the Angel of YHWH Alahim, who preceded the army of Israel, changed station and followed behind them. The pillar of cloud moved from their front to their back and took position behind them. (Exodus 14:3)

YHWH Alahim (Messengers/Angels) shaped man from the soil of the ground and blew the breath of life into his nostrils, and man became a living being. (Genesis 2:7)

YHWH took the man and settled him in the Garden of Eden to cultivate and take care of it. (Genesis 2:15)

There were certain sky beings who rebelled against YHWH's authoritative power and took to themselves the daughters of men, producing abominable offspring called Nephilim, whom humans worshipped as demi-gods. (Genesis 6:2, 4)

Table of Contents

CHAPTER 1

Self Help Culture

The power of the mind has been researched, tested, and also proven since ancient times. However, there was one particular people who used this knowledge at will to perform many miracles. In today's times, miracles still manifest themselves, but nothing comes close to the events that took place among the Hebrew people. Resurrection from the dead at will, the sun standing still for a day at will, sight to the blind, cure of disease and handicaps, parting of the seas and rivers, and telekinesis/astral projection.

He, for his part, went and presented himself to his master. Elisha said, "Gehazi, where have you been?" "Your servant has not been anywhere," he replied. But Elisha said to him, "Was not my heart (mind) present with you there when someone left his chariot to meet you?" (1 Kings 5:25–26)

The reason is that the Hebrew Israelite nation was founded upon the laws of attraction and the power of the subconscious and conscious mind. The Levite tribe was taken by YHWH as a special possession and was instructed with the duty of not only knowing the laws and performing the laws but to teach them to the people as well.

Of Levi he said: "They will teach your customs to Jacob, and your laws to Israel. They will put incense before you and burnt offerings on your altar." (Deut. 33:8, 10)

An entire nation of people was born and raised to know, understand, and perform according to these laws. The righteous ones protected the laws from outsiders who would misuse the knowledge for wicked and frivolous purposes.

And say this to the rebels of the house of Israel," the Master YHWH says this: "You who have gone beyond all bounds with all your loathsome practices, house of Israel, by the admitting of aliens uncircumcised in the heart (mind) and body to frequent my sanctuary and profane my temple. Instead of maintaining the service of my holy things, you have deputed someone else to maintain my service in my sanctuary." The Master YHWH says this: "No alien, uncircumcised in heart and body, may enter my sanctuary, none of the aliens living amongst the Israelites. (Ezekiel 44:6–9)

Do not give dogs what is holy, and do not throw your pearls in front of pigs, or they may trample them and then turn on you and tear you to pieces. (Matthew 7:6)

A nation, culture, and way of life dedicated to universal law! Chosen to be kings and priests to the world at large. Taught to place the principles of laws upon their hearts and minds, to write them on the doorposts of their homes and on their gates, and to teach them to their children. The reason for this is because the subconscious mind picks up everything the eyes and ears behold. This causes the repetitious download into the mind computer. Purposeful suggestion fills the mind and is projected back out into society and the physical environment and atmosphere of the people, for better or for worse.

This is why the societal laws were given, to keep man on a righteous path, treating each other as we would like to be treated.

You will not exact vengeance on or bear any sort of grudge against the members of your people, but will love your neighbor as yourself. I am YHWH. (Leviticus 19:18)

For example, a culture in which the people cut themselves in rituals and sacrifice their children, mark themselves, and commit immoral sexual activities will cause hurt and confusion to the physical and mental states of man. And this is how they treat themselves, so how do you expect them to treat you? Answer: they will rape you and your children, mark your flesh, cut you, and sacrifice your children, ultimately complying with the negative and/or regressive side of existence. For YHWH is the creator of both good and evil.

I form the light and the darkness, I create good and I create evil, I YHWH do all these things. (Isaiah 45:7)

An evil spirit from YHWH came over Shaul while he was sitting in his house with his spear in his hand. (1 Samuel 19:9)

However, the Israelite nation was founded upon the positive side of existence. They were taught to treat each other with respect and love for one another, and to be naturalists of the physical and spiritual realms.

YHWH spoke to Moses on Mount Sinai and said: "Speak to the Israelites and say to them: When you enter the land which I am giving to you, the land must keep a sabbath's rest for YHWH. For six years you will sow your field, for six years you will prune your vineyard and gather its produce. But in the seventh year the land will have a sabbatical rest, a sabbath for YHWH. You will neither sow your field nor prune your vineyard, nor reap any grain that has grown of its own accord, nor gather the grapes from your untrimmed vine. It will be a year of rest for the land." (Leviticus 25:1–5)

This is the true culture of the Israelites. This culture has been either forced or manipulated into inactivity among the Israelite tribes. Language, names, style of dress, and pattern of thought and action have been stripped from them by none other than themselves, by way of the adversary Shatan, the negative side of existence, as a result of the constant negligence of positive thought and the application of naughty behavior, breaking the covenant that was agreed upon between YHWH and the Israelites.

Jacob has eaten to his heart's content, Yeshurun, grown fat, has now lashed out. He has disowned the Alahim who made him and dishonored the Rock, his salvation, whose jealousy they aroused with foreigners; with things that are detestable they angered him. (Deuteronomy 32:15–16)

Be careful not to forget YHWH your Alahim by neglecting his commandments, customs, and laws which I am laying down for you today. When you have eaten all you want, when you have built fine houses to live in, when you have seen your flocks and herds increase, your silver and your gold abound and all your possessions grow great, do not become proud of heart. Do not then forget YHWH your Alahim, who brought you out of Egypt, out of the place of slave labor; who guided you through this vast and dreadful desert, a land of the fiery snake, scorpions, thirst; who in this waterless place brought you water out of the flinty rock; who in this desert fed you with manna unknown to your ancestors, to humble you and test you and make for you a happy future. Beware of thinking to yourself, 'My own strength and the might of my own hand have given me the power to act like this.' Remember YHWH your Alahim: He was the one who gave you the strength to act like this, thus keeping then, as today, the covenant which he swore to your ancestors. Be sure: if you forget YHWH your Alahim, if you follow other Alahim, if you do serve them and bow down to them, I testify to you today, you will perish. (Deuteronomy 8:1–19)

The Israelites drew to themselves conflicting nations who would then carry out the Israelites' worst fears here in the physical realm, which is why YHWH told the Israelites through Moses not to forget YHWH and not to mingle with or take up residence with certain nations of people.

Mark then, what I command you today. I am going to drive out the Amorites, the Canaanites, the Hittites, the Perizzites, the Hivites, and the Jebusites before you. Take care you make no pact with the inhabitants of the country which you are about to enter, or they will prove to be a snare in your community. (Exodus 34:11–12)

These people were terrible and threatened the way of life of the Israelites. The culture was to be protected from misuse, which is one of the reasons Gentiles were not allowed into the Holy of Holies and were prohibited from marrying into the nation of Israel in earlier times.

The seven days were nearly over when some of the Yehudi from Asia saw sight of him in the temple and stirred up the crowd and seized him, shouting, 'Men of Israel, help! This man is the one who preaches to everyone against our people, against the law and against this place. He has even profaned this holy place by bringing Greeks into the temple.' They had, in fact, previously seen Trophimus the Ephesian in the city with him and thought that Paul had brought him into the temple. (Acts 21:27–29)

The YHWH says this: No alien, uncircumcised in heart or body, may enter my sanctuary, none of the aliens living with the Israelites. (Ezekiel 44:9)

The culture has been stolen, misused, and used against the children of Israel by Gentile nations whose way of life advocates for the negative side of existence. The Hebrew Israelite nation must reclaim their identity by accepting who they are and also the responsibility they agreed to.

In Hebrew writings, there is an angel which governs every facet of existence: Angel of Air, Angel of Fire, Angel of Water, Angel of Earth, Angel of Healing, Angel of Emotion, Angel of Deception, Angel of Death, Angel of Sight, Angel of Love, Angel of Protection, and the list goes on. Humans worshipped these angels, and as time passed, man became even more lost as they began to worship objects that represented the attributes of their liking, due to the knowledge of the angels' attributes.

Any man who was fascinated with sight would worship the eagle or owl. A man who was fascinated with nature would worship trees, stones, or bodies of water (rivers/lakes). A man who was fascinated with sex or birth would worship the fertility goddess, which was represented by animals with high volumes of sexual activity such as the hare or rabbit (Easter holiday). These men and women would center their beliefs and family structure around these ideals and forms of worship, then develop new cults (cultures), which would last even until the present day.

According to the Bible, Seth, the son of Adam, would be the first to call upon the name of YHWH, who stands alone as the creator of all things that exist. Abraham, who was descended from Seth, would revive the ancient beliefs of Seth and become known as the father of monotheism, and as a result, the Hebrew Scriptures would become the foundation of all the world's major religions, giving birth to Catholicism, Christianity, Islam, Buddhism, Satanism, Talmudism, Judaism, and many more.

How, we ask ourselves, do so many different variations of belief come from one source of origin and have such drastic differences in doctrine? The rebellious nature of man is the answer and usual culprit. However, we have to keep in mind the possibility that there is a linguistic barrier between nations, and without true and proper understanding of ancient cultures and archaeological discoveries, our attempts to translate and interpret fall short of exactness.

When we take into account the fact that the Euro-Gentile community are converts to the Hebrew culture and were restricted from higher levels of sacred knowledge *"YHWH Alahim says this: No alien, uncircumcised in heart and body, may enter my sanctuary, none of the aliens living amongst the Israelites." (Ezekiel 44:9)* we find that teachings, whether genuine or malicious, are not 100% correct, causing a domino effect of false teachings and misunderstandings. The answer is to simply go back to the source.

As the children of Israel were scattered around the world, they took the truth with them, for they are the priests of the world according to the Bible. If we really want to know the truth, the best thing to do would be to ask the descendants of the true tribes of Israel.

Truth is, the name YHWH cannot be defined in exactness, as the Ein-Sof, which sits atop the Tree of Life, is defined as limitless and undefinable—Light.

CHAPTER 2

The Importance of the Family Structure

Imagine a beautiful House, perfect in all its dimensions and equipped with every feature imaginable: high ceilings, pool, vegetable garden, oakwood floors, chandelier, vintage style winding staircase, library, office, etc., everything you would like your Home to have according to your liking. Now, imagine the House infested with termites, eating away at the framework of the house, undetectable to a person with an untrained eye. The House represents our World, the Planet Earth, and the Termites represent the Human Species. We, the people, are eating away at the infrastructure of our beautiful Home, not only physically but also socially.

To fix our planet, we must simply restrain ourselves from voluntary pollution and mining of unnecessary resources. However, our social dilemma is the root of our physical issues. So, before we can fix or heal our world, or allow our World to fix itself, we must first fix ourselves. And it all starts with the reorganizing and correction of our Family Structure.

Families are what make up our social environment. Churches, schools, universities, etc., are all different types of families. In fact, in each of the aforementioned families or groups, positions are held by each member of the Family. There are rules and regulations for the proper and orderly running of the Family. The creator of the Family determines how the Family operates. The forerunner of the group allows input from members of the family as to any suggestions on how to make things run smoothly, which is wise.

However, the forerunner takes the suggestions into consideration and makes the final decision, for He or She is the Head of the organization. For every creator, there is a creation; for every top, there is a bottom, and so on. There are a Head, Body, and Tail of every organization. The Head is the MIND and INTELLECT, the HEART is the battery that keeps the body running, and the rest of the body parts have their own roles to play.

The chain of command begins with the MIND, which gives instruction to the body. Example: In a military outfit, a new recruit has to learn and experience combat skills, basic medical techniques, and leadership skills. If the Private learns and displays these skills effectively, He or She can move up the ranks into a higher position: Sergeant, Lieutenant, Captain, etc. If a Private with absolutely no military training were placed into the captain's position, he would most likely make a pretty lousy Captain. If the outfit is to run at an elite level, a qualified Captain is its best shot. If we add to those qualifications the scientifically proven fact that leadership is oftentimes genetically inherited, then you end up with world leaders such as Gandhi, Chaka Zulu, Adolf Hitler, and others.

Moses was the leader of the Israelites, as ordained by Yah to bring the Israelites out of Egypt. However, while in the wilderness, Moses became overwhelmed by the people's needs and disputes. Moses' father-in-law Jethro, the Priest of Midian, gave Moses wise counsel about the organization of people by rank.

The next day Moses sat to judge the people, and the people stood around Moses from morning till evening. When Moses' father-in-law saw all that, he was doing for the people, he said, "What is this that you are doing for the people? Why do you sit alone, and all the people stand around you from morning till evening?" And Moses said to his father-in-law, "Because the people have come to me to inquire of YHWH. When they have a dispute, they come to me, and I decide between one person and another, and I make them know the statutes of Yah and all His laws."

Moses' father-in-law said to him, "What you are doing is not good. You and the people will certainly wear yourselves out, for the thing is too heavy for you. You are not able to do it alone. Now obey my voice, and I will give you advice, YHWH be with you. You shall represent the people and bring their cases before YHWH. And you shall warn them about the statutes and the laws and make them know the way in which they must walk and what they must do. Moreover, look for able men among the people, men who respect YHWH, who are trustworthy and hate a bribe, and place such men over the people as chiefs of thousands, of hundreds, of fifties, and of tens. And let them judge the people at all times.

Any great matter they shall bring to you, but any light dispute they shall decide themselves. So, it will be much easier for you, and they will bear the burden with you. If you do this, YHWH will direct you, you will be able to endure, and all these people will go to their place in peace." So, Moses listened to his father-in-law and did all that he said. (Exodus 18:13–24)

This was sound advice which Moses followed, because in order to have a successful campaign there must be order, and all the leaders of the ranks must be qualified to lead. Thus, righteousness, honesty, integrity, and obedience are the qualifications that YHWH looks for in a leader.

The first social environment man comes into contact with is the immediate family, for they are the root of the community. The mother, father, sister, and brother family unit is the foundation of our societies and is most important for physical, psychological, educational, and spiritual development. If a child grows up in a family where drug use, theft, anger, and jealousy are present, the child is much more likely to carry these attributes into a society and can possibly corrupt social organizations such as public schools and working environments, not to mention other people as well. These situations or attributes could very well result in school shootings, embezzlement from employers, drug trafficking, and sexually transmitted diseases. If we wish to fix these and other problems, we must first start with ourselves and how we raise our families.

According to Scripture, YHWH says that the Children of Israel are a special people whom He chose to be kings and priests of the nations, to live by the decrees and be an example for the rest of the world to follow.

YHWH called to him out of the mountain, saying, "Thus you shall say to the house of Jacob and tell the people of Israel: You yourselves have seen what I did to the Egyptians, and how I bore you on eagles' wings and brought you to Myself. Now therefore, if you will indeed obey My voice and keep My covenant, you shall be My treasured possession among all peoples, for all the earth is Mine; and you shall be to Me a kingdom of priests and a holy nation. These are the words that you shall speak to the children of Israel." (Exodus 19:3–6)

If Israel is in darkness, the world is in darkness. If in a state of righteousness, then the world will be in righteousness. As a result of Israel's disobedience, YHWH cursed Israel according to the conditional covenant YHWH made with Israel. (Deut. 28: All) Our families were destroyed as a result of socializing with foreign nations, an abominable practice of which YHWH warned Israel.

Take care, lest you make an agreement with the inhabitants of the land to which you are going, lest it be a snare in your midst. (Exodus 34:12)

This abnormal family structure was caused by YHWH in regard to violation of the covenant. Fast-forwarding into more recent times, we refer to a slave trader who was rumored to exist by the name of Willie Lynch. Willie Lynch was a slave trader who resided in the West Indies. He devised a plan to keep the slaves divided among one another and to remain subservient to their masters. His techniques resulted in putting the light-skinned slaves against the dark-skinned slaves, old against young, father against son, mother against daughter, and man against woman. Another technique was the reversal of the family structure, whereby the Hebrew male was ill-treated, beaten, hanged, castrated, and burned alive before the eyes of all his family, women, and children.

The Hebrew woman, in turn, raised her children to respect the slavers lest they meet the same fate as their fathers, brothers, and husbands who attempted to stand up for their families. Thus, the Hebrew male was brought down low from being the head of his household to now being the tail, while the Hebrew woman was treated with a tad more respect than the males were, which caused her to be respected as the head of the family or household over time.

My people, infants are their rulers, and women rule over them. (Isaiah 3:12)

The Willie Lynch letter also states that once applied, his methods would cause a psychological effect that would last for many generations, and that the mind has the ability to correct and re-correct itself if it comes into contact with a historical base. Therefore, the slave masters had to keep the slaves oppressed and also keep a watchful eye in the case of uprisings. A prime example is the success of Hon. Marcus Garvey and his U.N.I.A.

organization, which called for social, spiritual, and economic development of African Hebrew people in America and Africa as well, for independence as a nation.

The African and American Hebrews responded well to Garvey and his leadership. They invested in his import and export passenger travel streamline ship company. As a result of Garvey's success, the United States government developed what is known today as the F.B.I. and hired a man by the name of J. Edgar Hoover, whose main objective was to thwart Garvey's plans for independence. According to the CO-Intel Pro documents, Hoover stated that his main duty and rector of the F.B.I. was to stop the rise of a "Black Messiah" (Anointed Spiritual Leader) who possessed enough charisma to invigorate the Hebrew people into coming together as a nation and fighting for their freedom.

And just like the mythical Willie Lynch letter, Hoover's tactics for dismantling Black independence were the old divide and conquer routine, which is not mythical in any sense. This tactic was applied by the F.B.I. to dismantle the success of the U.N.I.A., the Black Panthers, and many other Hebrew organizations. The leaders of these organizations and others like them were slandered in regard to their character and motivation for assembly. They were shot and killed, framed for crimes that shattered their reputations as positive community leaders, and thrown into prison.

In the case of Stanley Tookie Williams, co-founder of the Los Angeles Crips street gang, Tookie changed his life and began to write children's books and advocate for positive change in his community. He used his position as founder of the Crips to his advantage and negotiated a truce between the Crips and Bloods in L.A., as well as in other countries. His philanthropic work brought about positive change. His conduct was recognized, and he was nominated for the Nobel Peace Prize.

Despite all of this, a Gentile by the name of Arnold Schwarzenegger had the opportunity, as California State Governor, to save Tookie from execution, yet he allowed Tookie Williams to be executed. This is a prime example of the American government's implementation of the Willie Lynch methods of systematic oppression and the F.B.I. tactics of preventing the rise of a Black Messiah who has enough influence to invigorate his people. If the children of Israel want to have peace and order in their own communities, they must find some historical base of knowledge in regard to the proper and orderly running of the immediate family unit so that the mind, thoughts, and actions of the people can correct and re-correct themselves.

The relationship between man and woman is evident around the world at large, as the man, according to the Hebrew Scriptures, is the dominating half of the parental aspect of the family unit. The woman's role is to support her husband, for whose and from whom she was created.

The man gave names to all the livestock, and to the birds of the heavens, and to every beast of the field. But for the man, there was found no helper. So, YHWH caused a very deep sleep to fall upon the man, and while he slept took one of his sides and closed up its place with flesh. And the side that YHWH had taken, he formed into a woman and brought her to the man. Then Adam said, "This at last is bone of my bones and flesh of my flesh. She is called Woman, for she was taken from man" (Genesis 2:20-23).

To the woman he said, "I will greatly multiply your pain in childrearing. In pain you shall bring forth children. Your desire shall be contrary to your husband, yet he shall rule over you" (Genesis 3:16).

However, these two are in partnership for creating and multiplying our species upon Earth.

So, YHWH created man in his image, in his image and likeness he created him: male and female he created them (Gen. 1:27). And YHWH blessed them and said to them, "Be fruitful and multiply, and fill the earth" (Genesis 1:28).

The man does the hard work of plowing the fields, and he carries the heavier loads to and fro, constructing the homes, as he is genetically structured to perform these tasks.

The woman is a hard worker as well, in regard to her physical strength and capability. She raises and gives birth to the children, and takes care of the home, and she is appreciated for her contribution. When a woman is pregnant with child, she is unable to perform heavy tasks, so it is the job of the male to provide for her and his children. His job is to protect her in her time of incapability in regard to pregnancy.

This systematic structure is designed by a power that created us! Have we no trust in the power that made us! A psychological game has been played against us once again, in relation to the Willie Lynch Syndrome, as the Hebrew woman has been put against her man and vice versa. When disputes arise in the home, the woman is more likely to tell her husband to "Get out, I don't need you," and they proclaim their independency. However, that independency is limited, and their dependence has only been transferred from the Hebrew male to the government agencies that provide healthcare, childcare, Medicaid, food stamps, etc.

The male is more likely to leave his family because he has little to worry about, knowing that his family will be taken care of by the same government that provides for them. The word "govern" is an ancient Latin word that means "control," and the word "ment" is an ancient word that means "mind" (Ment, Mental, Mente). Put the two words together, and you get "GOVERNMENT," or better yet, "mind control."

Though there did exist a barrier of inequality, the Hebrew woman was respected in Israel and held high positions in the community.

Now Deborah, a prophetess, the wife of Lappidot, was judging Israel at that time (Judges 4:4).

Then Queen Esther, the daughter of Abihail, and Mordecai the Yehudi gave full written authority, confirming this second letter about Purim. Letters were sent to all the Yehudim, to the 127 provinces of the kingdom of Ahasuerus, in words of peace and truth, that the days of Purim should be observed at their appointed times and seasons, as Mordecai the Yehudi and Queen Esther obligated them and their offspring, with regard to their fasts and their lamenting. The command of Esther did confirm these practices of Purim, and it was recorded in writing (Esther 9:29-32).

The Hebrew woman was respected and honored in family life as well as in business and commerce.

She makes garments and sells them. She delivers sashes to the merchants. Strength and dignity are her clothing, and she laughs at the time to come. She opens her mouth with wisdom, and the very teaching of kindness is on her tongue. She looks well to the ways of her household and does not eat the bread of idleness (Proverbs 31:24-27).

The Hebrew Torah consists of laws, statutes, commandments, and ordinances given to the Hebrew Nation for the purpose of instituting natural and moral values for social and communal environments. These righteous instructions are the spiritual building blocks for a peaceful social environment.

The Torah provides methods on how to repair damages caused to the structure by the natural elements of energy. Only YHWH knows how to correctly balance His existence and creation of positive and negative energies, so why is it that people fail so miserably when it comes to having trust in YHWH and His wonderful Torah? The Torah provides instruction for the purpose of proper maintenance of, and enjoyment of, the positive things that life has to offer. The answer is simply because our families have been coerced into confusion, abandonment, and disarray of YHWH's Laws, whether they be social or universal.

People around the globe have been led to believe that freedom to behave however you like is the fair way to exist: eat what you like, say what you like, worship whatever god you like, even wood and stone, or stars, trees, and animals. This liberal mindset is ridiculous and chaotic. Any believer of the Bible should take note that YHWH our Creator is indeed a dictator in the purest degree. YHWH set laws in place for us to abide by, or else we will reap the consequences of our actions. YHWH's laws are good for us, yet it is still a dictatorship. YES! YHWH does want us to obtain peace and prosperity, but we must do it His way and prove ourselves worthy of ascension by His judgment of our behavior.

The Serpent in the Garden taught mankind how to obtain higher states of consciousness by ways other than being obedient to YHWH and earning our favor. If certain spiritual gifts, ideals, or information fall into the wrong hands, they will be misused and abused, used carelessly and not carefully.

CHAPTER 3

Garden of Eden

And YHWH planted a garden in Eden, to the east, and there He put the man whom He formed. Out of the ground, YHWH Alahin made every tree grow that is pleasant to the sight and good for food, with the Tree of Life in the middle of the garden, and the Tree of the Knowledge of Good and Evil. A river went out of the place of Eden to water the garden, and from there it divided and became four riverheads.

The name of the first is Pishon. It is the one that surrounds the entire land of Havilah, where there is gold. And the gold of that land is good, and bdellium is there, and the shoham stone. The name of the second is Gihon. It is the one surrounding the whole land of Cush. The name of the third is Hiddekel. It is the one which goes toward the east of Asshur. And the fourth is the Euphrates.

And YHWH took the man and put him in the garden of Eden to work it and to guard it. And YHWH commanded the man, saying, "Eat of every tree of the garden, but do not eat of the tree of the knowledge of good and evil, for in the day you eat of it you will surely die" (Genesis 2:8-17).

When taking into consideration the creation epic, most people read this story in the literal sense, believing the garden to be some physical oasis only. There have been many souls searching for the treasures of the garden, where there lies the Tree of Life and the knowledge of good and evil. They seek fortune, fame, and recognition from their peers, with failed efforts time after time.

In this section, we will explore the garden, and we will use allegorical language to explain or compare the garden to the Law of Vibrations.

Starting with the first river, which flows from Eden into the YAH Garden as a "current of energy flowing into the higher consciousness from which Man originates." We must realize that from there (the Garden) four rivers (currents of energy) flow (Genesis 2:10). In all, totaling five rivers, which correlate to the five senses: sight, taste, hearing, smell, and feeling (touch). The water, which is the current of energy, represents that which causes life to spring up.

The first river flows into the Garden to water the trees: Knowledge, Life, Emotion, Feeling, Love, Humor, and all other attributes of Man and YHWH. Can you imagine experiencing life without consciousness? IT IS IMPOSSIBLE! So, let's get this straight: the river (energy) flows into Eden, and there in the Garden it then permeates the higher states of consciousness, watering the Garden, in which grows the Tree of Life (Conscious), which can only be fathomed with the use of the five senses.

From the Garden, four of the five senses (rivers) flow out. The reason only four rivers flow out is because there is one which is the foundation of them all. Imagine losing your five senses one at a time. First you lose your hearing. So, if you cannot hear, how will you know if someone is calling your name? Well, you might say you can still see them, right? Unless, of course, they are behind you. So, if they are behind you and you cannot hear them or see them, then maybe you can smell them, unless, of course, they are too far away or for some odd reason your sense of smell has failed you.

So, if they are too far away to smell, behind you so you cannot see, and you cannot hear them, how will you know the person is there? Well, some people might say, "I can just feel when someone is watching me; it is my intuition. I can just 'sense' them." Hypothetically speaking, if you lose taste, touch, hearing, smell, and feeling, you will be totally unconscious of what is going on around you. But will you still exist? Physically, yes!

And Alahim created man in His image, in the image of Alahim He created him, male and female (Genesis 1:27). And Alahim formed man out of the dust of the ground, and He breathed into his nostrils the breath/spirit (consciousness) of life (Genesis 2:7).

We see here that man existed, but he was unconscious until YHWH placed into his being the Spirit (consciousness) of life as a vibration or energy. In Hebrew, this Spirit or energy is now called the Neshamah.

Once the man came to life, knowing sight, taste, touch, and hearing, of which feeling encompasses them all, he was now aware of life. In the Hebrew scripture, oftentimes two verses correlate to each other, meaning that they are describing the same event as a continuing thought. Genesis 2:7-8 represents a good example:

...The man became a living being (he received conscious awareness) Genesis 2:7. There He placed the man whom He formed (He placed man into a Garden of conscious awareness) Genesis 2:8

The Garden of consciousness was available to the man at a level where he could have control of conscious attributes, which are governed by vibrational frequency. When man was removed from the Garden, he was prohibited from having complete control of his conscious mind in the Astral Realm.

There are two forces, Masculine and Feminine (not to be confused with male and female). When Shatan, which is the feminine or regressive force, intrigued the curiosity of Noman, she veered off the straight path of construction to entertain the regressive force of destruction.

And YHWH, the Will to Be, commanded the man, saying, "You may eat of every tree of the Garden, but of the tree of the knowledge of good and evil, do not eat" (Genesis 2:16).

And the serpent was more revealing than all the lives of the field which YHWH Alahim made, and he said to the woman, "Is it true that Alahim has said, 'Do not eat from all the trees of the Garden?'"

And the woman said to the serpent, "We are to eat of the trees of the Garden, but of the fruit (doctrine) of the trees (beings) which are in the midst of the Garden, Alahim has said, 'Do not eat (consume) of it or touch (entertain) it, lest ye die (be cast out).'"

And the serpent said to the woman, "You shall certainly not die. For Alahim knows that in the day you eat of it, your eyes shall be opened, and you shall be like Alahim, knowing good and evil."

And the woman saw that the tree was good for food, that it was pleasant to the eyes, and a tree desirable to make one wise, and she did take of its fruit and eat (Genesis 3:1-6).

When the man entertained the curiosity of evil, which is the feminine or regressive force acting with doubt, giving room for the regression of his conscious mind, it resulted in expulsion from the Garden. Although man can still see, smell, taste, touch, and hear, he has lost complete control and has been stranded in a restricted field of the lowest levels of reality. His doubt of his true nature represents the sword of flames to keep him away from his former position.

And He drove the man out, and He placed cherubim at the east of the Garden of Eden, and a flaming sword which turned every way to guard the way to the Tree of Life (Genesis 3:24).

The Five Senses

The five rivers in the creation epic parallel the five senses, which are all incorporated in the same source in Eden and in the Garden. It is only when the rivers stretch forth out of the Garden that they separate in different directions (Genesis 2:10).

The river that went out of Eden into the Garden is not named, and this first river represents the sense of **Feeling**, because Feeling is the nature of, and/or in relation to, the conscious mind, which in its essence is the senses combined.

Touch/feeling

This is the foundation of the senses. Everything moves; nothing is still. What appears to be solid matter is actually movement vibrating at lower rates, depending on the density, size, color, shape, and position of an object. These attributes all contribute to the vibrational rate of any particular object, or perhaps the vibrational rates contribute to the attributes. This is why different things feel different, including your emotions. You can literally "feel your mood change" because your emotions are solid matter vibrating at different frequencies, being output by the mind, which we as individuals have been taught will dictate what or how we should feel in certain situations. Therefore, our thoughts, which are vibrations, contribute to or make up the components of the conscious mind, "the senses." Vibration and motion are the first river and the most important "river" which "flows" out of Eden, the Garden of Consciousness.

Hearing

Sounds are vibrations, depending on the tone, pitch, and range, as well as the fluctuation of a specific sound. Languages are identified by these vibrations. A human voice, controlled by our conscious mind, can be used to change pitch and tone to mimic the voices of others. Hearing is feeling sounds produced by thought. Sounds move at slower or faster rates, bouncing off objects and reflecting in different directions.

Smell

Smells are vibrations and are substances that vibrate at specifically designed frequencies. You cannot see them with the naked eye, but they are indeed substances, and they travel from one place to another. They can become attached to you and cause you to smell like them. If you go into an airtight room with no wind circulating, and open the lid of a freshly baked apple pie, you will smell the pie because the nature of all things is movement. The smell vibrates on its own and pushes its scent throughout the room. Depending on the strength of the vibration, the smell can travel certain distances. Wind can carry the smell further. Smell is a physical, tangible substance that vibrates and relates to "Taste".

Taste

Taste and smell are related because we can taste what we smell. Your nose breathes in the smell and transmits it to the tongue, which registers it as a specific flavor to the kind or thought.

Sight

Eyes are sensors. Colors, textures, and shapes output specific vibrations. This is why our eyes, as sensors, identify different objects as distinct from each other according to random combinations of matter. Our eyes are the original telescopes, designed by YHWH, the highest power and creator of all things, and are extremely powerful. Considering the owl or eagle, we have learned through observation and scientific research that an owl can adjust its eyes willingly to see at night in various nocturnal settings. The eagle flies high above the earth, yet it can use its eyes to see its prey from extremely high altitudes, for example, rodents moving on ground level. Our thoughts use our eyes to determine "sense," the vibrational output of objects, similar to the dolphin.

When man was removed from the Garden, he lost control of the senses as a unified force. The river that went out of Eden represents the senses again as a unified force. Further along the river, it comes to the Garden, from there it divides into four rivers and separates the power of the unified forces. While man was in the Garden, he was to have access to the power of unity.

When a man loses his hearing, one or maybe all of his other senses may be heightened. Imagine being able to heighten any of your other senses without losing another. How about raising your sense of hearing without losing your sight? Musician Ray Charles lost his sight when he was very young. As a result, his sense of touch, smell, and hearing were greatly enhanced. He trained himself to survive depending on his remaining senses. Imagine if man could enhance all of his senses on command; he would be considered superhuman. Or imagine purposely suppressing one sense in order to enhance another. This rare technique is used in martial arts, where a student is blindfolded and trained to rely on his remaining senses to determine when an opponent is striking, from where, and how fast. Once the blindfold is removed, the skill of the student is much more efficient than ever before.

The man was instructed not to eat of the Tree of the Knowledge of Good and Evil and to eat only of the trees that produced good fruit. He ignored his good sense and ate of the negative or regressive fruit, which is doubt, causing unsurety and instability of the unified forces.

When a parent instructs a child to do or not do something, and explains to the child the consequences and repercussions of defying the command, and the child does not take heed, the child is ignoring his Good Sense, submitting to doubt. The child feeds the Dog, holding his hand out to the Dog's mouth. The Dog then bites the child along with the food that was in the child's hand, and the child is now hurt and crying. The child wishes he did not ignore the command of his Parent. The Parent then says to the child, have you lost your mind, have you any "Good" Sense?

To be unconscious is to be unaware, and to be unaware means that you have lost your Mind (Spirit).

A Hebrew word may have several meanings which are determined by the context in which it is used. RUACH, Blow, Breathe, Smell, "Perceive," Anticipate, Enjoy, Wind, Region of the Sky, (Spirit, but only of a rational being including its expressions and functions), Make of quick Understanding. NESHAMAH, Puff, Wind, Angry vital Breath, Divine Inspiration, "INTELLECT," An Animal Blast, Inspiration, Soul, Spirit.

As we can see from the above definitions, the understanding of the creation story in the Hebrew writings is much clearer than ever before. When consulting the Hebrew Scripture, we find that in Genesis 2:7, YHWH Alahim blew into the nostrils of man the Neshamah, Divine Inspiration or Intellect, which is made up of the Senses and is the essence of awareness.

And the Man Adam became a living being. To be alive is to be aware, or in other words, conscious. The Neshamah is the combination of all Senses and creates a unified force of awareness, capability, and creativity directly connected to YHWH.

In Genesis it reads, "all in whose nostrils was the breath of life, all that were on the dry land died." JPS Tanak

"All in whose nostrils was the breath of the spirit of life, all that was on the dry land died." I.S.R. Scripture translation.

In the JPS version it says Breath of Life, however in the I.S.R. version it says the Breath of the Spirit of life.

According to the Hebrew script, the I.S.R. version is most accurate with the addition of the word Spirit.

With the Hebrew words Neshamah, Ruach, and Chayim being written in that order, a proper translation would be:

All in whose nostrils was the Neshamah (Divinely Inspired), Ruach (Mind), of Chayim Life (Awareness, Conscious), and all that was on the dry land died.

And this is understanding of the Garden of Eden, in part.

CHAPTER 4

Force/Sound Vibration

Force Sound Vibration, which resonates throughout all that exists. When YHWH the creator of all things tangible decided to bring or manifest itself into what we know as solid matter, the energy produced a sound, and that sound and energy manifests itself into all things seen and all things unseen. When specific sounds are produced through a means of whatever origin, they can be heard or felt by Man or any living being by the use of the mechanical device we know of today as ear drums. If by chance a being is not at all equipped with traditional ears or its ears have failed to work properly, the beings rely on the sense of feeling, which is in its essence hearing in an alternate form.

Blind people have been known to differentiate between a five-dollar bill and a one-dollar bill, because each bill weighs a separate amount. The vibrational output is dependent upon the structural makeup of the bill, i.e. thickness of paper, cotton, amount of ink, type of ink, etc. Therefore, the blind person can tell by the vibrational output which bill is which. The key principle behind it all is vibration. The Dolphin, being a perfect example, uses a much larger percent of its brain than a human does. The Dolphin produces sound waves which reflect off of all objects in a measured radius and brings back to the Dolphin the specific output of vibration from all objects in the area. The dolphin does not hear the Shark coming, at least not in the traditional sense, they feel it which is in its essence hearing.

When an object is in its original state it will produce its own core language. Language can be a single sound or a vibrational output or even a combination of sounds strategically orchestrated by the mind of a conscious being. With sound or language, being pitch, range or a combination of both, it can be smooth, rough, attractive or unattractive, it can be magnetic or repulsive to the eyes of the beholder. However, there are vast amounts of generally attractive or unattractive frequencies in existence.

The Man, being created in the image and likeness of the creative life forces, also being blessed with the will to decide, has the ability to himself create. Therefore, he can create that which is deemed constructive or destructive.

Sound is raw energy which can surely be manipulated for better or for worse, depending on how you perceive it. Man can mimic the sounds of other people, Animals, Objects, or Elements to the point where it could be hard to actually determine the real from the fake. Mariah Carey, the singer songwriter, has been known to sing at such a high pitch that she could cause glass to break with the mere sound of her voice. Or how about comedians who make funny noises with the express intent to change drained and boring environments into funny and uplifted atmospheres. They can do so willingly with sound being the key element in all of the above examples. It shows how sound can affect or even manipulate people, places and things. Also keeping in mind that force is the essence of sound and sound is in relation to motion.

Beauty and Poetry are synonymous terms which denote what is attractive, not only in the traditional sense, but also Felt, Heard, Smelled and Tasted. All five of the senses are receptors and detectors of any one and or various force vibrations. A good example of a generally attractive quality is the scent of a fresh baked Apple Pie bursting with the aroma of Ginger, Cinnamon and Brown Sugar. It can be described as a plate full of Poetry for the senses to enjoy!

Atmosphere may be best described as the condition of any environment, be it physical, Visual or Emotional. A perfect example of such an environment is the Human Body. The body can be sickly or healthy, tired or upbeat, worn, beaten or shiny and polished and in tip top shape. The condition of the said environment determines the emotional state of the person which can be Sad, Happy, Disdainful, Reluctant, Angry, Humorous, Loving or Hateful. With the Mind being its own environment, having an atmosphere of its very own, Man can be placed in an already conditioned environment and unknowingly take on or adapt to the attributes of its atmosphere. For example, we as free willed beings have the choice to either change, adapt to, or remain neutral in any environment we encounter. As evidenced, a Man can change the atmosphere in a room, or the atmosphere in a room can change a Man due to lack of awareness. To again become attuned to the natural vibration we were born with could be the doorway to the desired state of Gnosticism we are all searching for.

The collective attitudes of a nation of people determine states of atmosphere in which they live. There are plenty of examples of neighboring cities, whereas one of the cities is filled with crime and violence, and the conditions of poverty at rates much higher than the other city. Both cities have Policemen, Shelters, Food Drives, Mayor, Governor, Schools, City Council, etc. Yet still each city maintains a completely different atmosphere. When a Pedestrian passes from the safe city into the Dangerous City, they are more likely to adjust to the environment of the city in which they are headed. They check the locks on the doors to make sure they work well. They might wear gang neutral colours for the purpose of avoiding conflict, drive a less expensive vehicle to avoid car jackers. Maybe they will bring a registered handgun for protection, proceeding with a nervous aura and ultimately attract to themselves the same unwanted attention they fear most.

This works the same in reverse while traveling from the dangerous city and entering into the safer city. This same pedestrian now let's down his windows, turns up the Music, moves the handgun from the glove department to the trunk, puts the blue hat he loves to wear back atop his head and lets out a sigh of relief. As we see from the above example, the atmosphere of an environment can be detrimental to the behavior of the people who dwell within it.

Poetry

Poetry would be best described as a feeling to be experienced by the senses of a conscious being. Traditionally, poetry has been known from ancient times as a blissful experience, or by today's standards as words put together in patterns that produce rhythmical outcomes. This same method was used in ancient times. Poetry is also the feel of soft furry Animals for all those who enjoy that feeling, for beauty is in the eye of the beholder. A beautiful canvas painting of a horizon with a rising sun could be poetry to the Mind through the use of the eyes. The smell of that fresh baked Apple Pie would be poetry to the Mind through the use of the nose by sense of smell. And the Sound of a musical orchestra would relate to the sense of hearing. Sound or Force is the essence of all things created, therefore Poetry in the form of Music has been very influential in the process of times unfolding.

Most people know that the Hebrew Prophets delivered the messages in the form of Poetry. Hebrew Scripture writings such as Psalms, Songs of Solomon, Proverbs and also Ecclesiastics are known to be poetical writings. However, all major and minor prophets are also poetical writings, this fact is lost amongst the many translations of the Scriptures into foreign tongues. Therefore, the seeker must embrace the original language and writings in order to get a true understanding of Hebrew culture from ancient times. Scribes would traditionally place poetry into scripture and indicate it by placing a blank space or mark in each section whereby the rhythm or poem is to be presented.

The very ideal of poetry and prophecy should be examined by all who believe in the Bible or any offshoot of it. The city of Yerushalem is described to be a haven of golden Streets, Walls, Pearls, Rubies and Self-Sufficient essence of light and Marvelous Structure. (Rev 21:18-27). It only makes sense that YHWH would converse in the most beautiful and extravagant way known to Man, "Poetry" or "Song".

The Hebrew people who are dear creations to YHWH the Most High would be sure to take on attributes or traits similar to their creator. In Hebrew culture the poetry was used to deliver Prophecy, Express Love, and Admiration for someone or something and also, it was used to apply a Curse or Blessing. In some instances, the blessing would be delivered through a minor prophet for persons, places or things. Men or Women would also apply personal Curses or Blessings upon their children for either praised or ill conduct.

(HE SAID "CURSED BE CANAAN: THE LOWEST OF SLAVES SHALL HE BE TO HIS BROTHERS. AND HE SAID, "BLESSED BE YHWH, THE POWERS OF SHEM: LET CANAAN BE A SERVANT TO THEM. MAY YHWH ENLARGE YEPHETH, AND LET HIM DWELL IN THE TENTS OF SHEM: AND LET CANAAN BE A SERVANT TO THEM" Genesis 9:25-27)

(YOU O YAHUDAH, YOUR BROTHERS SHALL PRAISE YOUR HAND SHALL BE ON THE NAPE OF YOUR ENEMIES; YOUR PATHER'S SONS SHALL BOW LOW TO YOU. YAHUDAH IS A LION'S WHELP ON PREY, MY SON, YOU HAVE GROWN. HE CROUCHES, HE LIES DOWN LIKE

A LION, LIKE A KING OF BEASTS WHO DARE ROUSE HIM? THE SCEPTER SHALL NOT DEPART FROM YAHUDAH, NOR THE RULER'S STAFF FROM BETWEEN HIS FEET: SO THAT TRIBUTE SHALL COME TO HIM AND THE HOMAGE OF ALL PEOPLE BE HIS. (Genesis 49:8-10)

The Ismaelites who are Hebrews as well have indeed kept this poetic culture. During the times of the Prophet Muhammad the most revered and respected Men in Arabic society were poets. The better the recital the more respect. When researching Hebrew scripture, we can see each moment where the poetry was used in the above references. This style of poetry is a reoccurring theme in curses and blessings. In modern times it is used to Enhance Memory, Induce Sleep, etc. When we really think about it, it is present in conjuring spells in séances, in the traditional scary movie there is usually the voice of a woman or child reciting a song or poem which is frightening in nature, with maybe a group of hooded individuals standing around in a circle swaying in rhythm to a spell that has been created from demonic poetry.

The Hebrew bible is a historic record of a special nation of people who had no so called advanced technology for the purpose of recording and saving data to be later reviewed at their leisure. Instead, they used the original and most powerful computer known to Man "The MIND". They downloaded oral history through poetry and song, because it is always easier to remember things through Songs. The American Slaves of the trans-Atlantic Slave Trade would sing songs about Zion while working in the fields which were passed down from ancient times. In all cultures and religious sects' devout members use Song, Poetry or Chanting (THEN MOSES AND THE ISRAELITES SANG THIS SONG TO YHWH. THEY SAID: I WILL SING TO YHWH, FOR IT HAS TRIUMPHED GLORIOUSLY: Genesis 15:1)

ALL THESE WERE UNDER THE CHARGE OF THEIR FATHER FOR THE SINGING IN THE HOUSE OF YHWH BY ORDER OF THE KING. ASAPH, YEDUTHUN, AND HEMAN, THEIR TOTAL NUMBER WITH THEIR KINSMAN, TRAINED SINGERS OF YHWH, ALL THE MASTERS, 288. (1st Chron. 25:6,7) From the repetitive chants of the Asian cultures to the song and dance of the African and Native American Tribe, rhythm and poetry were and still are heavily present.

(NOW THEN GET ME A MUSICIAN, AS THE MUSICIAN PLAYED, THE HAND OF YHWH CAME UPON HIM, AND HE SAID, THUS SAYS YHWH:

2nd Kings)

Entertainers use music to express Love, Fear, Bravery, Pride, Religion and support amongst a people down trodden. A universal outlet shared around the world by all nations and Languages. According to scripture, YHWH our power enjoys rhythm and song so much so that there is a very special breed of Angels created specifically for this desire.

(REV. 14:3)

The world at large is at present a victim of mass hypnosis as a result of the Musical background of everyday life and outlets of Media and Entertainment. Seemingly such an innocent art, it is always there looking in the distance. Those with understanding know the Khazarian Jews who control the World Banking System, News Media and Entertainment Industries use Music to manipulate the Minds of the watcher and listener. It has been prophesied in the Hebrew Scripts about the sons of Yapheth, sons of Yawan Greeks, that would enslave the Israelites in the latter days. These Ashkenazis were also prophesied to dwell in the "Tents of Shem" seemingly replacing the true Sons of Shem in the position of the light of the world, only the Yephethites would rule by the iron fist of mental and physical chattel slavery.

The effect of hypnosis is most easily conjured by the swaying of objects in rhythmic motion and the sound of a monotone voice repeating a chant or song in a very special and seductive manner. These tactics are used every day on unsuspecting large masses of people through television and radio. The Sub Conscious Mind is attacked repeatedly using subtle suggestion, Mannerisms, Colors, and Music, being the most powerful element and weapon of choice, from TV ads, Folk Songs, Movie Soundtracks, National Anthems, College Bands and Fraternity Initiations, etc. All the way down to the Ice Cream Man who rides around urban areas all across the U.S.A. while playing music filled with bells and whistles catering to the attention of little boys and girls who can at times hear the music from several blocks away.

For example, there is a mom and pops store directly across the street from a family of a single mother and two children ages nine and eleven. The children enter the store on a daily basis and strut past the same brands of Ice Cream being sold on the Truck. It is often when the children hear the sound of the music blasting from the Ice Cream Truck that all of a sudden something clicks in the Mind of the children and there is now a craving for Ice Cream, the same brand of Ice Cream the mother could have purchased from the store for such a cheaper price just ten minutes earlier.

This method of hypnosis is being applied unknowingly every day around the clock. When watching Movies, the graphic in the movie along with the best scriptural dialogue just does not have the same effect without the musical soundtrack to go along with it, as it takes watchers on the musical emotional roller coaster throughout the duration of the film. There is a genre of music to go along with every emotion: Fear, Excitement, Pain, Anticipation, Acceptance, etc. By the end of the film the Movie watcher has been taken and emotionally manipulated to feel exactly the way the film's producer wants them to feel.

Ask yourselves, if an uplifted and exciting soundtrack is applied to a morally unclean and filthy sequence of events, would the movie watcher become confused and begin eventually to believe that morally obscene behavior is also uplifting and exciting? The answer is an astounding YES. Especially with children.

During a deeply emotional scene the feeling of pain and suffering rushes over a person like a wave of energy as the eyes begin to water. Right before the tears fall, right in the very middle of the scene, grab your remote control and put the TV on mute and witness first hand the change in your own personal atmosphere as the tear ducts dry and emotion subsides.

A classical Orchestra takes the listener on the same emotional roller coaster only there are no actors, scripts or enhanced graphics to go along with the music, there are just the musicians and their instruments. It was always the Music that was the dominating factor behind the film, this includes the voice and mannerisms of the actors. We are now being controlled through music emotionally, the sound, poetry, and sub conscious suggestions.

The Ashkenazi Khazars are imposters of the true children of Israel and are in control of the sacred brotherhoods who impose the "Protocols of the Learned Elders of Zion" upon not only the real Israelites, but the world at large. The true children of Israel shall think to apply and embrace ourselves with the sounds which induce us to reembrace our original culture and break away the bonds of mental and emotional slavery placed upon us by our oppressors.

We should think to gather the strength to remove ourselves from the atmosphere of this gentile rule. We are engulfed in idol worship, ie. Sports Trophies, Plaques, Paper Currency, Statue Hollywood Walk of Fame, Jewelry, also Automobiles, Modern Day Pillars, Sky Scrapers and Music Awards which are miniature Idols, AMA's, Grammy, Oscar, B.E.T. Awards, VMA's, etc.

The true Children of Israel are victims of a classic case of "world wide Pimpin". We work for the government and give all of our earnings back to the government through Tax, Lottery, Traffic Fines, Medical, and Incarceration Fees, just to name a few. The Hebrew American spending statistics is billions and we are the minority in the United States.

Our own sovereign land and private schools that teach agriculture and self dependency is what we need. We need land and connections in other countries to prepare for mass Exodus. The fight for acceptance has crippled our reliance upon each other and now we rely on outside entities for our very means of survival.

Dr. King seemed to have the right ideal; however he fell victim of the Protocols. The Dr. King holiday is a secret dedication to the death of our independence as a nation of people. It is no wonder why they gave him a nationally recognized holiday. Malcolm X died in the same tragic manner as Dr. King, yet Malcolm was fighting for our people's independence through sovereignty. Do you see the difference? Where in the world is Malcolm's nationally celebrated Holiday? Marcus Garvey? Ben Ammi?

As for the Power of Poetry and Music, the Khazars know and understand it and use it against us with conscious intent. In the beginning of the Hip Hop era, the artists made music with the intentions of uplifting the people in slums, impoverished ghettos and neighborhoods. The big record executives who are Ashkenazi Khazars signed new artists to contracts giving them celebrity fame, yet robbing them of millions of dollars and dictated the lyrical content of the records to be released. As a result, the music went from Afrika

Bambaataa and the Zulu Nation, Grandmaster Flash and Public Enemy, to a mode of Gangsta Rap which would feed into the Sub Conscious causing anger, violence and foolishness.

If you control the atmosphere, you can control the Mind and emotions of the people. The Khazars are aware of the musical culture of the ancient Hebrews and the power of poetry. Those who have eyes to see and ears to hear, and also the Mind to investigate the truth behind this information, will make the effort to reembrace the appliance of positive vibrations into the atmosphere with the express intent to change it for the better. Though we have grown to love our folly, we must recognize it for what it is, and we should make the sacrifice and give it up for the greater good. To deprogram the Western mindset, the beginning of the deprogramming is contingent upon realizing who you are as a Nation of people. Investigate the vast differences of the cultures in different places around the world, a few examples: When two people become married in the U.S., they are allowed to divorce and then remarry, and do this numerous times over and again, even after the woman has defiled herself with another husband.

However, Hebrew Israelite Law (YHWH's Law) says that after a woman has divorced her husband for another and lies with the new husband, she can no longer join in union with her former husband. You can have only one wife in the U.S., but in the Middle East and in Africa, you may have as many wives as you like, depending on your capability to take care of the responsibilities that come along with that way of life. Have you ever noticed how couples get married in the U.S., and the minister seals the union with this statement: "By the power invested in me by the state of, let's say, Mississippi, I now pronounce you man and wife"? They do not even use the word God; they give all the credit to the state. Let's ask ourselves what happened to the power of the Highest YHWH.

Socializing: In the Western world, you have beaches where people parade around in basically nothing, in front of small children and the elderly alike. Can you imagine a man wearing only a speedo cruising past your young, impressionable child, grabbing his crotch as he lusts after a woman whose private parts are protruding through her swimsuit? In a Hebrew or even a Muslim country, this type of behavior would be frowned upon. These types of situations are typical in the West and are in opposition to YHWH's Law. In order to reclaim our true identity, we must remove the Western influence and reclaim our culture, language, and sense of self-worth.

It all starts with education. The school systems of America purposely teach our children and adults how to destroy themselves physically and mentally by mixing truth with falsehood. For instance, the public schools in urban areas teach mathematics but only a primitive curriculum, while most schools in Caucasian-dominated areas teach far more advanced courses. History, as we all know, has been fabricated in both Ibriw and white schools, teaching young children that Ibriw people came to America on slave ships, which is true. However, they conveniently leave out the fact that Rebrew people were already here. This is evidenced by the memoirs of Christopher Columbus when he landed in the West Indies; he took slaves from the Americas back to Europe, and the captives were classified as "Negroes."

We as a nation must rediscover who we are and take back our original laws and customs as they were given to us by the Hebrew Prophets. YHWH reinstituted the Law to a new nation, which He chose to rise up from the seed of Abram. The new nation was to adopt the customs of the universal laws of YHWH and occupy His chosen land. The original inhabitants of the land profaned YHWH's laws, and as a result, those peoples were rejected by YHWH and replaced by the children of Israel, who were used as a tool in the hand of YHWH to remove the rebellious peoples (Deut. ch.7).

When studying the laws and customs of the inhabitants of the African continent, we find that many of the customs of the tribes reflect Hebrew Israelite traditions that reach back into the antiquity of the tribes, such as Sabbath observance, priestly duties, style of dress, language, and more. This secret knowledge of who the Hebrews are has been hidden from the true Hebrews. Let us recall the period of chattel slavery, when Hebrew slaves were prohibited from learning to read and were penalized if they were caught being too smart.

During this period of history, many European scholars and historians wrote essays and papers about the true history of the Negroes. Of course, if the slaves knew how to read, they would have become aware of the truth of who they are. The identity of the Hebrews was stolen, and they were forced to believe they were inferior through forced religious beliefs, physical abuse, and massacres of the people. The only way to repair the damage that has been done is to reclaim the position that was given to them as priests of the world and to embrace the laws and customs of YHWH, bringing the message of the Way of Life to the nations of the earth.

Many movements have arisen to invigorate the people to migrate back to Africa to establish the rights and respect of the people worldwide. This was attempted by Marcus Garvey, Delany, and other lesser-known Black activists. However, it seems these efforts have always been prohibited from accomplishing their goals successfully, with the exception of Ben Ammi Bin Israel, an American-born Israelite who successfully migrated from the Americas to Israel along with around 350 devout members of his congregation during the Civil Rights era.

Upon further inquiry of the Hebrew congregations of the Americas and throughout the world, victims of the Trans-Atlantic Slave Trade have been proclaiming themselves to be the lost sheep of Israel, spoken of and historically documented since the days they stepped off the ships into the Western world. The overall mission of the Hebrews is to reclaim the laws, statutes, and commands instituted in the Hebrew scriptures. It is important to note that the laws given to the people of Israel through the prophets are universal. For example, if a person eats an unclean animal such as clams, shrimp, or oysters, they will become sick. The average person responds to such a statement with, "My grandmother ate pork all her life and lived to be one hundred," as if one hundred years is a long life.

Humans consume the worst narcotics, such as ecstasy, cocaine, and heroin. We become sick or disoriented immediately, yet after years of abuse, our bodies seem immune to the drugs, and it takes more consumption to achieve the same effect as the first indulgence.

The worst condition of slavery is the present-day condition of Hebrews in America, who believe they are free but are actually mentally enslaved, having no idea of the matter. The same goes for dietary laws, where people consume poisonous and filthy animals, contributing to numerous health issues without realizing that the foods they consume are the primary cause. The vast majority of people living on the continent of America have been sculpted into the model of the varying satanic governments in control. Through television, music, radio, sports, and various other media outlets, people have been directed to eat certain foods, drink certain beverages, and even walk and talk a certain way. In sum, the controlling authorities get you to think the way they want through subliminal messages and subtle hypnosis. Once the first domino falls, the rest of history follows.

The government teaches Mark, who teaches his son that it is okay to respect the rights of homosexuality, who in turn teaches his daughter the same, who then engages in an intimate relationship with another woman. This couple then adopts a child, who grows up in the middle of a demonically possessed household, having no understanding of the fact that their parents are in direct opposition to the laws of nature. This cycle continues until such behavior seems normal.

This is a call to all mankind to recognize and repent from transgressions of YHWH's natural and universal laws and reclaim the natural "rhythm of life." Parents can take the time to investigate the history of our ancestors thoroughly and homeschool their children. Teach the children that it is not okay to disrespect husbands or wives, and teach them that it is not okay to destroy their bodies with toxins such as alcohol, marijuana, ecstasy, and other drugs, which are obvious instruments of self-destruction.

Now, let us examine some of the less obvious toxins, such as lotion, hair grease, shampoo and conditioner, aspirin, cough syrup, tap water, artificial sweeteners, saccharin and aspartame, bleach, washing detergent, cologne, perfume, food coloring, and preservatives. Judging by this list, we can deduce that the average person wakes up in the morning, brushes their teeth, showers with soap, rubs lotion into their skin, applies hair grease, sprays fragrance, takes over-the-counter prescription drugs, dresses in clothes washed with chemicals such as bleach and detergents, and sits down to a breakfast filled with saccharin, aspartame, food coloring, and preservatives, most likely prepared in a microwave oven that produces radiation. Heating the aspartame beyond recommended limits transforms it into a dangerous chemical compound that can cause brain disease. From the moment a person wakes up until they leave their home, they have consumed hundreds of chemicals, and that is just the beginning of the day. The problem is that the negative effects of these chemicals often go unnoticed because of daily use.

Since we come into the world as small children, our parents, taught by controlling authorities through various media outlets, have used these products on us and themselves. It is no wonder that by the age of fifty, we have become victims of numerous diseases such as cancer, diabetes, tooth decay, STDs, Alzheimer's, asthma, ADD, gingivitis, AIDS, and many more. I am not saying that we should not groom ourselves, but we should be more careful of the products we use and always check labels for hazardous ingredients.

Let us be more selective and start looking for more organic products, natural foods, medicines, and cleansers. The Western world has even made it illegal to grow organic produce and sell it without their consent. The U.S. government sued a woman for selling her own organic seeds rather than purchasing the government's non-reproducing genetically engineered seeds. We must return to the natural universal laws of YHWH, respect one another, speak to each other in truth, raise our children to be leaders structured according to the laws of YHWH, and deprogram our minds from the ways of Western influence.

CHAPTER 5

Idol Worship Vs. Intended Purpose

Idol worship consists of any created object worshipped by Man for its attributes or even its sentimental value. YHWH tells us not to worship any created object; however, using the object for its intended purpose does not mean we are worshipping it. If the inhabitants of Earth quit building homes with wood and stone, stopped shepherding sheep for wool, and ceased drinking water to live, then man's time on Earth would be a million times more painful than our already unwise decisions have caused us to experience.

SUN - Beginning with the Sun, it is a tool used by YHWH for several purposes, many we know and many we have yet to understand. What we do know is that the rays which emanate from the Sun strengthen melanin, provide vitamins and minerals, and give us light to see along with warmth and revitalizing energy. These elements nourish the Earth, the plants, and animals, including Mankind.

MOON - The Moon is the master of boundaries. It holds in place the tides of the rivers, lakes, and seas. It gives light to see at night, amongst other useful works. Both the Sun and Moon are essential to dwellers of this planet we call Earth and provide for us a way to keep time.

AND ALAHIM MADE TWO GREAT LIGHTS: THE GREATER LIGHT AND THE LESSER LIGHT, THE GREATER LIGHT TO RULE THE DAY & THE LESSER LIGHT TO RULE THE NIGHT, AND ALSO THE STARS. AND ALAHIM SET THEM IN THE SPACE OF THE HEAVENS TO GIVE LIGHT ON THE EARTH, AND TO RULE OVER THE DAY AND THE NIGHT, AND TO SEPARATE THE LIGHT FROM THE DARKNESS. (Gen 1:16,17)

However, we are not to become so awed by the attributes of these heavenly bodies that they cause us to err by worshipping them and bowing down to them.

IF I HAVE LOOKED AT THE SUN WHEN IT SHINES OR THE MOON MOVING IN BRIGHTNESS, SO THAT I AM ENTICED BY THEM SECRETLY IN MY HEART, AND MY MOUTH HAS KISSED MY HAND, THAT TOO IS PUNISHABLE CROOKEDNESS, FOR I WOULD HAVE DENIED AL ABOVE. (Job 31:26,27)

WHEN THERE IS FOUND AMONG THE MUST OF ANY OF YOUR CITIES WHICH YHWH YOUR ALAHIM IS GIVING YOU, A MAN OR WOMAN WHO DOES WHAT IS EVIL IN THE EYES OF YHWH YOUR ALAHIM, IN TRANSGRESSING ITS COVENANT, AND HAS GONE AND SERVED OTHER MIGHTY ONES AND BOWED DOWN TO THEM, OR TO THE SUN OR TO THE MOON OR TO ANY HOSTS OF THE HEAVENS WHICH I HAVE NOT COMMANDED, AND IT HAS BEEN KNOWN TO YOU AND YOU HAVE HEARD AND SEARCHED DILIGENTLY. (Deut 17:2,3)

STONE - Depending on the species of stone, the healing properties they contain vary. Rocks and stones clean and provide minerals in streams, lakes, and rivers. Stones are also used for shelter, tools, communication, and monetary value. As far as communication goes, there are certain types of stone that, when struck, produce melodies that can be heard over vast distances. Melodies and tunes have been used for such things as approaching danger, storm alerts, meal time, and more. Precious stones have been used to portray idols in sculpture. A few examples of Stones and the attributes associated with them are:

- **Emerald** - Associated with healing of the kidneys and liver, and connection with the third eye Chakra.
- **Moon Stone** - Cools the body, releases energy, increases intuition, and its power is said to change with the Moon's phases.
- **Amethyst** - Increases meditation by way of high vibration, a wide spectrum of healing energy, and balances the crown Chakra and third eye Chakra.
- **Ruby** - Master of gems, warms the body, increases physical energy and leadership skills, and is associated with the Earth Chakra.
- **Gold** - As for gold, it is used for its most widely known attribute of monetary value; however, it is also used for its durability in space travel (elasticity) among other uses.

- **Diamonds** - Diamonds are also used for monetary value, though they are also used to harness energy and for cutting in workmanship.

It is no wonder why Israel fell victim to the worship of stone. To worship any stone and bow down to it as a sculpted or unsculpted idol is a transgression of YHWH's laws. However, using these stones for their intended purposes is not worship. Even the Levitical priests were commanded to place certain gemstones into the set-apart breastplate of righteousness.

AND YOU SHALL MAKE A BREASTPLATE OF RIGHTEOUSNESS, A WORK OF A SKILLED WORKMAN, LIKE THE WORK OF THE SHOULDER GARMENT. MAKE IT OF GOLD, BLUE, PURPLE, AND SCARLET MATERIALS AND FINE WOVEN LINEN. IT IS SQUARE, DOUBLED, A SPAN ITS LENGTH, AND A SPAN ITS WIDTH. AND YOU SHALL PUT SETTINGS OF STONES IN ITS FOUR ROWS OF STONES: THE FIRST ROW IS A RUBY, A TOPAZ, AND AN EMERALD; AND THE SECOND ROW IS A TURQUOISE, A SAPPHIRE, AND A DIAMOND; AND THE THIRD ROW IS A JACINTH, AN AGATE, AND AN AMETHYST; AND THE FOURTH ROW IS A BERYL, A SHOHAM, AND A JASPER. THEY ARE SET IN GOLD. (Exodus 28:15-20)

Staff of Moses - When the children of Israel were in the wilderness during the exodus from Egypt, they were stung by serpents of the desert. As a result, Moses gave the staff to be looked upon by all those afflicted, that they might be healed.

AND YHWH SENT FIERY SERPENTS AMONG THE PEOPLE, AND THEY BIT THE PEOPLE. AND MANY OF THE PEOPLE OF ISRAEL DIED. THEN THE PEOPLE CAME TO MOSES AND SAID, "WE HAVE SINNED, FOR WE HAVE SPOKEN AGAINST YHWH AND AGAINST YOU. PRAY TO YHWH FOR US TO TAKE AWAY THE SERPENTS FROM US." SO, MOSES PRAYED ON BEHALF OF THE PEOPLE. AND YHWH SAID TO MOSES, "MAKE A FIERY SERPENT, AND SET IT ON A POLE. AND IT SHALL BE THAT EVERYONE WHO IS BITTEN, WHEN HE LOOKS UPON IT, HE SHALL LIVE." SO, MOSES MADE A BRONZE SERPENT AND PUT IT ON A POLE. AND IT CAME TO BE, IF A SERPENT HAD BITTEN ANYONE, WHEN HE LOOKED AT THE BRONZE SERPENT, HE LIVED. (Numbers 21:6-9)

This staff, which belonged to Moses the prophet of YHWH, held enormous sentimental value to the Israelites, for they loved Moses in addition to the miracle of health that was associated with it. And so, they worshipped the staff.

AND HE DID WHAT WAS RIGHT IN THE EYES OF YHWH ACCORDING TO ALL THAT HIS FATHER DAVID DID. HE TOOK AWAY THE HIGH PLACES AND BROKE THE PILLARS AND CUT DOWN THE ASHERAH AND BROKE IN PIECES THE "BRONZE SERPENT" WHICH MOSES MADE, FOR UNTIL THOSE DAYS THE CHILDREN OF ISRAEL BURNED INCENSE TO IT AND CALLED IT "NEKUSTAN." (2 Kings 18:3,4)

Groves/Trees - DO NOT PLANT FOR YOURSELF ANY GREEN TREE AS AN ASHERAH NEAR THE ALTAR OF YHWH YOUR ALAHIM THAT YOU MAKE FOR YOURSELF. AND DO NOT SET UP A PILLAR WHICH ALAHIM HATES. (Deut. 16:21,22)

Trees, depending on the species, have many benefits. They produce sap. They are used to build homes and bridges, and they protect us from the sun in extreme temperatures by providing shade. Trees also produce oxygen, which we breathe in for life-sustaining energy. The above list is only a few of the benefits of trees. With all of these wonderful attributes, it is no wonder how the Israelites fell victim to worshipping trees as idols. YHWH clearly hates any idol worshipped in its place.

THESE ARE THE LAWS AND RIGHTEOUS RULES WHICH YOU ARE TO GUARD TO DO IN THE LAND WHICH ALAHIM OF YOUR FATHERS IS GIVING YOU TO POSSESS, ALL THE DAYS THAT YOU LIVE ON THE SOIL. COMPLETELY DESTROY ALL THE PLACES WHERE THE NATIONS WHICH YOU ARE DISPOSSESSING SERVED THEIR MIGHTY ONES ON THE HIGH MOUNTAINS AND ON THE HILLS AND UNDER EVERY GREEN TREE. AND YOU BREAK DOWN THEIR ALTARS AND SMASH THEIR PILLARS AND BURN THEIR "ASHERIM" WITH FIRE. AND YOU SHALL CUT DOWN THE CARVED IMAGES OF THEIR MIGHTY ONES AND SHALL DESTROY THEIR NAME OUT OF THAT PLACE. (Deut. 12:1-3)

SIX POINT STAR - The Six Point Star has been rumored to have been worshipped by King Solomon through his foreign wives and has been called a pagan symbol. However, considering the explanations of intended purposes, the Six Point Star only becomes pagan when it is worshipped. Like anything else created, it has its purposes. Man can use this tool only if he understands how to use it correctly.

A tool of spiritual science, the star appears when a certain vibration is produced. Sounds are vibration and vibrations are sound. Specific tones bring into this realm the Six Point Star, or is it that the Six Point Star brings into this world specific vibrations? The star represents the principle of the oneness of duality, as does the symbol of Yin and Yang. Harmony, duality, the fabric of existence, celestial science, and understanding of various manifestations on this vibrational plane of existence are all contained here. YHWH has allowed this understanding in part only amongst earthly man. The Philistine deity Ashtoreth is the same deity said to have been worshipped by Solomon under the influence of his foreign wife.

AND SOLOMON WENT AFTER ASHTORETH, THE MIGHTY ONE OF THE TSIDONIANS, AND AFTER MILKOM, THE ABOMINATION OF THE AMMONITES. (1 Kings 11:5)

If you return to YHWH with all your heart, then put away Ashtoreth from among you, prepare your hearts for YHWH, and serve Him only, so that He delivers you from the hand of the Philistines. (1 Samuel 7:3)

"We see in front of us the result of complex periodic vibration, a musical tone becoming a 'visible' figure in which one or more intervals are featured. One must always bear in mind that these phenomena are generated by sound. If the sound is removed, the whole picture along with its dynamics will disappear and return immediately when the sound is restored. These phenomena are subject to definite laws and are repeatable at any time. The resultants of harmonic vibrations are at all times so strictly law-ordered that it is possible to draw up a systematology of morphogenesis. What one must bear in mind is that under this or that quite specific set of conditions, Nature produces this form only and no other. Nothing here is diffuse and indeterminate: everything presents itself in a precisely defined form. The more one studies these things, the more one realizes that sound is the creative principle. It must be regarded as primordial." Hans Jenny, Cymatics, 2 vols., 1974, Basilius Press, vol. 2, p.106.

We as a people are not to bow down to, praise, or glorify the symbol; however, there is an intended purpose for its existence. When YHWH blesses an individual with the knowledge, wisdom, and understanding of that purpose, it is up to the individual to use the element accordingly without being lured into worship. Those who have ears to hear and eyes to see, may it be so.

AND ELISHA SAID, "AS YHWH TZEBAOT LIVES, BEFORE WHOM I STAND, IF IT WERE NOT THAT I REGARD THE PRESENCE OF YAHOSHAPHAT, SOVEREIGN OF YAHUDAH, I WOULD NOT LOOK AT YOU NOR SEE YOU. AND NOW BRING ME THE HARPIST." AND IT CAME TO BE, WHEN THE HARPIST PLAYED, THAT THE HAND OF YAH CAME UPON HIM. (2 Kings 3:14,15)

ANGELS

The intended purpose of the Angel is to do service for all that exists. In the Book of Enoch, many angels and their attributes are disclosed to Enoch. These messengers deliver the petitions of Man to our creator, YHWH. To invoke these messengers is not worship unless, of course, a man bows down to them in worship and in place of YHWH. To use or ask the angels for some particular thing according to their intended purpose is quite alright, though one must keep in mind the insight of underlying issues, such as the Fallen Angels who taught Man the science of alchemy, weaponry, and herbal medicine, which is evil in the eyes of YHWH for the Malachs in this regard.

To ask yourselves, "Why would the science of herbal medicine be evil in the eyes of YHWH?" is a very good question and of much worth. For the herbs heal or prevent sickness and health problems. The understanding is this: there are many levels of existence, from the highest field of vibration of the spiritual world down to the lowest vibrational field of the physical world.

When Man (Adam) fell from the world of spirits to the world of physical form, he could no longer depend on the concentrated power of Conscious Mind at all of its various levels to nourish and maintain himself. By being a part of the physical world, he now has to rely on physical world-created things. It was never the intent of YHWH for Man to fall; however, Man has the ability to choose (free will), and the Fallen Ones (Angels) allowed jealousy to fester within them on account of YHWH's adoration of Man. They then caused Man, by way of deceit, to choose to rely upon physical objects, which was evil in the eyes of YHWH. Those who have the Spirit of understanding will see!

The universal laws of creation have a divine plan, which involves an opportunity for mankind to reach higher states of consciousness, to be like or one with the power that created them if found worthy. As for the maintenance of the garden, Man has failed miserably at his job and has kindled anger and backlash from the creative forces. Ancient Asian, African, and Native American cultures all have doctrines of wisdom and understanding in relation to creation and spiritual science. However, the Hebrew Way of Life always stands out amongst the rest, with simple and easy-to-understand indisputable facts that place elements of Hebrew culture amongst all cultures and nations in the world.

("Have you found the beginning that you are looking for the end? For where the beginning is, there the end will be. For blessed is the one who will grasp the beginning: he will know the end and will not experience death.") Gospel of Thomas 18

Enoch lived 65 years and brought forth sons and daughters. He brought forth Methuselah, and after he brought forth his son Methuselah, Enoch walked (abided by the word of YAH) 300 years and did not taste death, for he was taken by YHWH. Genesis Ch. 5 of the Hebrew scriptures

CHAPTER 6

Power of the "Collective".

A man of YHWH can defeat 1,000; two can put 10,000 to flight. (Deut. 32:30) Two heads are better than one! United we stand, divided we fall! Where two or more are gathered in His name, He is present!

The above sayings and scriptures are just a few of the many that attest to the power of numbers. In regards to the minds of men, ideas reach substance faster and more effectively when individuals come together and "brainstorm" the ideas presented. There is a transference of energy from one mind to another, which picks up that "vibe" and builds upon it. As long as each participant shares the same beliefs and goals and remains on one accord, the chances of success and manifestation are great.

As evidenced by the Hebrew Scriptures, YHWH advocates for His children to be on one accord and of like mind. The power of the collective is key to the creation process, and we can use this number's power in our own lives. Think about a multi-billion-dollar corporation dealing with the same types of products and services. Each of the differing corporations holds a board meeting wherein the top executives, owners, managers, and investors come together as a collective body to "brainstorm" ideas to effectively reach possible consumers through advertisement, etc. Seldom, if ever, will you find a successful business operated by one person.

There is always a partner involved, a group of employees, an investor, a test friend, or a spouse who inspires ideas in the mind of the owner. Remember what the Apostle Paul says in the New Testament about the Body of the Anointed:

AND TO SOME, HIS GIFT WAS THAT THEY SHOULD BE APOSTLES; TO SOME, EVANGELISTS; TO SOME, PROPHETS; TO SOME, PASTORS; TO SOME, TEACHERS; TO KNIT YHWH'S HOLY PEOPLE TOGETHER FOR THE WORK OF SERVICE TO BUILD UP THE BODY OF THE ANOINTED. (Ephesians 4:11,12)

That's right! Each member of the collective has his or her own special field of expertise, and when each attribute comes together as one, as a force of positivity, it creates an environment of excellency. Just as the organs in the body of man have distinct functions yet work together as one to facilitate the necessary maintenance of man's existence in this physical realm.

Each mind in the meeting of the minds must be on one accord, and everything flows smoothly. It is only when negative thoughts creep into the 'mind meeting' that the possibility for the collapse of positive progress manifests. In the business of creation, YHWH is the only mind responsible for the initial thought of the business of existence.

THE PRINCE OF THE KINGDOM OF PERSIA HAS BEEN RESISTING ME FOR TWENTY-ONE DAYS, BUT MICHAEL, ONE OF THE CHIEF PRINCES, CAME TO MY ASSISTANCE. (Daniel 10:13)

This scripture is of the Angel Gabriel speaking to Daniel about the fallen angel who opposed him. For if the Prince of Persia were a man, Gabriel would not have needed the assistance of the Angel Michael to help subdue him (Prince of Persia).

YHWH created Michael; Michael created Gabriel, and together they created the remainder of the archangels. Thus, the executive branch of the business of creation was born. Among this group of executives was Lucifer, the Bright and Morning Star. Business was well until the creation of man, at which point Lucifer became jealous. The hatred of the new creation invaded his positive nature and caused disruption in the affairs of the business. As a result of his rebellious behavior, YHWH, who is the creator of all and owner/operator of the corporation, demoted Lucifer and removed him from the heavenly executive order of angels, sending him to rule over the Asiyah world of solids, liquids, and gases related to the Earth planet.

Since then, Lucifer has attempted to influence as many souls as possible to spread negativity throughout YHWH's creations until he could possess enough shares in the corporation to cause a hostile takeover.

CHAPTER 7

The Festive Observance

In the Book of Enoch (Bk. 3:72-82), it is revealed to Enoch the workings of the Sun and Moon throughout the year at an intricate level, explaining how the first half of the year our days grow longer and the night becomes shorter until the midway point of the year, then the pendulum swings the other way, causing the nights to grow longer and the day to become shorter. Every six months, this celestial clock's pendulum of shadow and light begins to swing in the opposite direction. Shadow and light, and bad and positive, forward and backward, masculine and feminine, Yin and Yang.

Though these are opposites, they work together to weave the fabric of existence. Without light, can there be dark?

WHEN YOU COME INTO THE LAND WHICH I GIVE YOU, AND SHALL REAP ITS HARVEST, THEN YOU SHALL BRING A SHEAF OF THE FIRST FRUITS OF YOUR HARVEST TO THE PRIEST. AND HE SHALL WAVE THE SHEAF BEFORE YHWH, FOR YOUR NATION'S ACCEPTANCE. ON THE MORROW AFTER THE SHABBATH THE PRIEST WAVES IT. (Lev. 23:10,11)

According to these passages, the Hebrews were instructed to reap the harvest of the land and wave the sheaf on the day after the Shabbath, which is on the day of Passover. This means that the waving of the sheaf and grain offering is on the first day of Unleavened Bread. The Passover is on the 14th day of the month.

AND YOU DO NOT EAT BREAD OR ROASTED GRAIN OR FRESH GRAIN UNTIL THE SAME DAY THAT YOU HAVE BROUGHT AN OFFERING TO YOUR POWER. (Lev. 23:14)

Let us not lean on our own understanding, and let us study to show ourselves approved, for the answer is present in scripture.

AND THE CHILDREN CAMPED IN GILGAL AND PERFORMED THE PASSOVER ON THE 14th DAY OF THE MONTH AT EVENING ON THE DESERT PLAINS OF JERICHO. AND THEY ATE OF THE STORED GRAIN OF THE LAND ON THE "MORROW AFTER THE PASSOVER," UNLEAVENED BREAD AND ROASTED GRAIN ON THE SAME DAY. (Joshua 5:10-11)

As we can see here, the Israelites are just now entering the land of promise, and they performed the Passover and ate of the stored grain of the land the day after the Passover, which is the first day of the feast of Unleavened Bread. This is another confirmation that the Passover is performed on the 14th day of the month (the Shabbath).

The entire chapter of Exodus 16 explains how the Israelites grumbled against Moses and Aaron on the 15th day of the second month after they came out of Egypt. The Israelites were to gather the manna on the 15th, 16th, 17th, 18th, 19th, 20th, and 22nd day of the second month, with the 21st day being the Shabbath. Let us ask ourselves: if the 14th day of the first month is a Shabbath and the 14th day of the second month is a Shabbath, then would it be safe to say that the 7th, 14th, 21st, and 28th day of every month is a Shabbath? Let us agree that there are 30 days in a month. Would the two or three extra days be the New Moon celebration as a period of separation between one month and another? (In different cultures, a monthly period is counted differently. For example, the Islamic month is 28 days.) For if you count from the 28th day of the first month, it would go as follows: 28th day (Shabbath), 29, 30, 1, 2, 3, 4, and 5, with the fifth day being the seventh day Shabbath, which would be inconsistent with Ex. 16.

AND ALAHIM SAID, "LET LIGHTS COME TO BE IN THE MIDST OF THE HEAVENS TO SEPARATE THE DAY FROM THE NIGHT, AND LET THEM BE FOR SIGNS AND APPOINTED TIMES, AND FOR DAYS AND FOR YEARS, AND LET THEM BE FOR LIGHTS IN THE MIDST OF THE HEAVENS TO GIVE LIGHT ON THE EARTH." AND IT CAME TO BE SO. (Gen. 1:14,15)

These passages explain how the lights in the expanse of the heavens are to be used for signs, appointed times, days, and years. The Shabbath is one of those days (appointed times).

When the Gregorian calendar is removed from the existence of thought, and the true and natural application of observance by way of the heavenly bodies (Sun, Moon, and stars) is followed, then the appointed times will shine forth like light out of darkness! Remember, YHWH said that we would forget our culture and heritage as a result of our disobedience.

(ALSO, OUR SHABBATHS AND APPOINTED TIMES) AND NOW I SHALL CAUSE ALL HER FESTIVALS, HER NEW MOONS, HER SHABBATHS, EVEN ALL HER APPOINTED TIMES, TO CEASE. (Hoshea 2:11)

Many congregations claim to observe YHWH's laws the correct way, yet many of these groups differ from one another. Let us remember that YHWH is not the author of confusion, and there is only one true way, and that is YHWH's way. To find the truth, we will consult strictly with the scriptures and put aside all emotions and feelings for the teachings of men.

The count starts at the first sighting of the Moon (the first crescent), which represents the first day of the month. Then you count seven days, which puts the seventh day as the Shabbath day. Seven days later, we come to the fourteenth day, then the twenty-first, and lastly the 28th day is the fourth Shabbath, ending the monthly cycle of four Shabbaths, bringing the month to an end and starting the New Moon festival and renewal of the Shabbath cycle.

The Sun reflects light upon the Earth and works harmoniously with the Moon as our clock so that we know when to observe our appointed times. YHWH is merciful and understands the conditions we are faced with, so He gave us statutes of atonement for those who sin by mistake.

....AND DO NOT DO ALL THESE COMMANDS WHICH YHWH HAS SPOKEN TO MOSES, ALL THAT YHWH COMMANDS YOU BY THE HAND OF MOSES, FROM THE DAY YHWH GAVE THE COMMAND AND ONWARD THROUGHOUT YOUR GENERATIONS, THEN IT SHALL BE, IF IT IS DONE BY MISTAKE, WITHOUT THE KNOWLEDGE OF THE CONGREGATION, THAT ALL THE PEOPLE SHALL PREPARE ONE YOUNG BULL AS A BURNT OFFERING, AS A SWEET FRAGRANCE TO YHWH, WITH ALL ITS GRAIN OFFERING AND ITS DRINK OFFERINGS ACCORDING TO THE RIGHT RULINGS, AND ONE MALE GOAT AS A SIN OFFERING. THEN THE

PRIEST SHALL MAKE ATONEMENT FOR ALL THE PEOPLE OF THE CHILDREN OF ISRAEL, AND IT SHALL BE FORGIVEN THEM, FOR IT WAS BY MISTAKE.... (Numbers 15:22-25)

CHAPTER 8

The Power of Sacrifice

SACRIFICE: To give up something in order to receive something else in return; to give something of value, sentimental or personal, for the benefit of someone else.

Typically, sacrifice is associated with giving up something you love or hold dear. To be unselfish with belongings or certain relationships allows the mind to have room for blessings we would not otherwise receive due to our extreme focus on specific objects. The more we love the game of golf or basketball, if we spent less time playing the sport, we would have more time to build relationships with our loved ones. This could lead to a long-lasting relationship, a happy and fulfilling marriage, etc. If we take inventory of our lives and the things that matter most to us, the usual list would go as follows for our top five:

1. Family
2. Career
3. Health
4. Hobbies
5. Other

These are at the top of just about everyone's list; however, we often spend more time watching TV, playing video games, playing sports, going out to parties or clubs, overeating, or going to amusement parks. We continue to spend time and money on leisure activities that do not profit us. If we could just "sacrifice" half of what's on our leisure list, we could spend more time and energy on our top five.

Try adding up how much money you spend on soda pop, party favors, bottled water, fancy restaurants, Christmas gifts, expensive clothing, etc. Per year, we spend thousands of our hard-earned dollars. Now, think about this: if we save every penny and give up the things which are unnecessary for about two years, we would have enough money to start our own businesses and probably wouldn't have to work for the rest of our lives, unless of course we were working for ourselves depending on what we choose to pursue.

The time we spend on non-important activities could be spent on educating our children, meditating, and getting in tune with our own personal energy. This brings us to the inclusion of sacrifice in the Hebrew Israelite self-help culture.

Sacrifice has taken place from the earliest points of biblical history, from the days of Adam up until the days of Moses and beyond. But how or why is sacrifice necessary?

The answer is because YHWH understands the nature of man and his inclination to hold dear the created thing as opposed to the creator of those things. And so, YHWH demands the sacrifice of what we love most to free our minds from the chain of physical reality. YHWH gives an example with the test of Abraham and the request to sacrifice his son Isaac.

WHEN THEY ARRIVED AT THE PLACE WHICH YHWH HAD INDICATED TO HIM, ABRAHAM BUILT AN ALTAR THERE AND ARRANGED THE WOOD. THEN HE BOUND HIS SON (ISAAC) AND PUT HIM ON THE ALTAR ON TOP OF THE WOOD. ABRAHAM STRETCHED OUT HIS HAND AND TOOK THE KNIFE TO KILL HIS SON. BUT THE ANGEL OF YHWH SAID TO HIM FROM HEAVEN, "ABRAHAM, ABRAHAM!" HE SAID, "HERE I AM," HE REPLIED. "DO NOT RAISE YOUR HAND AGAINST THE BOY," THE ANGEL SAID. "DO NOT HARM HIM, FOR I KNOW YOU REVERENCE YHWH. YOU HAVE NOT REFUSED ME YOUR OWN BELOVED SON." THEN LOOKING UP, ABRAHAM SAW A RAM CAUGHT BY ITS HORNS IN A BUSH. ABRAHAM TOOK THE RAM AND OFFERED IT AS A BURNT OFFERING IN PLACE OF HIS SON.

(Genesis 22:9-13)

There's an old saying that goes, "*We must give in order to receive.*" Only if we knew how true this saying is, then we would practice it more often. There is a catch to it all: we must give freely without expecting anything in return.

I give you an example of a drug addict who is homeless and hungry. He is asking for food or a few dollars, maybe. Will people encountering this person pass him by, thinking to themselves, "*Geez, this guy is begging again; he has already wasted his own money on drugs. I'm not going to let him waste mine as well. I worked hard for my money, and I'm not giving him a damned thing!*"

This mode of thinking is uncompassionate. Who knows why this person is on drugs in the first place? It could have been caused by abusive relationships, being an army war veteran with PTSD, mental disability, or sexual abuse as a minor. The drugs could be his way of coping with disastrous happenings in his life. Remember the time you needed a helping hand and a complete stranger came to your aid. Then you caught a flat tire and you did not have a spare; a stranger came along and gave you his own spare or a lift to a service station or auto shop. Or how about if you invested in a company that soon after went bankrupt and you were on the verge of losing your home. A friend or family member came to your aid asking nothing in return except that you make wiser decisions in the future.

Let us be careful of how we judge others, for the measure with which we judge, we will be judged also. Let us sacrifice our selfish desires, self-centeredness, haughty behavior and useless idolatry of anything that is not our Creator itself. This brings us also to the Shabbath Day observance as it is also a sacrifice of our everyday activities that we love to do. On the Shabbath rest we are told to do no work and to praise our Creator in a set apart gathering and to do invocation. We have become accustomed to making money, doing trade and business and construction work.

At the time of the same I saw people in Jerushalem in Yahudah treading the winepress, bringing in sacks of grain and loading donkeys on the day of the Shabbath. They were also bringing wine, grapes, figs and every kind of merchandise which they were selling to the Yahudites on the Shabbath in Jerushalem itself. So, I also reprimanded the leading men of Yahudah, saying to them, "*What a wicked way to behave on the Shabbath Day, profaning it. Was this not exactly what your ancestors did with the result that our All brought all this misery upon us and on this city? And now you are adding to the wrath hanging over Israel by profaning the Shabbath yourselves.*" So, when the gates of Yahrushalem were getting dark at the approach of the Shabbath, I gave orders for the doors to be shut and directed that they were not to be opened again until the Shabbath was over. (Nehemiah 13:15 to 19)

YHWH prohibits these acts so that man can have time for his mind to rest along with his body for concentration on his spirituality and meditation on YHWH's laws. The Shabbath is an extremely important observance for those who understand this weekly sacrifice of our worldly desires. This is the day we free our minds from the congested traffic of information and let our subconscious take in information, requests and orders that our desires be processed and manifested into our lives.

Fasting. Fasting is also synonymous with sacrifice because we must give up our physical nourishment to allow our minds and bodies to heal themselves. There have been in recent times people who claim that fasting is unhealthy because of the lack of vitamins and mineral nutrients we get from the foods we eat. Studies have shown that the intestines of the average person are being overworked. The liver, kidney, heart and pancreas are essential to the proper running condition of not only the body but of the mind. People who fast regularly tend to be healthier, and if they become sick with disease, they heal much faster than usual because the organs of the body are not busied with processing and breaking down foods consumed, giving the organs the opportunity to perform other tasks effectively.

Fasting prevents clutters of waste from being built up in our system. Ultimately these clutters of waste can cause a sort of traffic jam which prevents the nutrients from doing their job. At times it can also cause an overload of nutrients with the result of a backfire that can result in heartburn, gas, vomiting, clogged arteries, clogged pores, colon cancer, hemorrhoids, irregular fecal distribution, loss of concentration and focus of the mind and the list goes on.

Fasting allows the body to extract nutrients properly and purge itself of toxins allowing for a clean and properly running machine. This is great for our health, body and mind. During a fast people often have better concentration and keener senses which make for stronger prayers.

CHAPTER 9

Meditation In Scripture

An art of concentration on any area of existence that is fathomable by the petitioner. The meditative art is associated largely with Asian cultures such as Chinese, Japanese, East Indian and so on. Though meditation is present in scripture, the practice is avoided by some preachers who explain it away as whoring with the practice of foreign doctrines.

Upon reading the scriptures we find that meditation was and still is a vital part of Hebrew culture, as our forefathers such as Issac and others practiced this art.

AND ISSAC WENT OUT TO MEDITATE IN THE FIELD IN THE EVENING. AND HE LIFTED UP HIS EYES AND LOOKED AND SAW THE CAMELS COMING. (Genesis 24:63)

In the Book of Jasher, the members of the Twelve Tribes were recorded as performing what is considered to be amazing and impossible feats such as lifting huge boulders, running at unbelievable speeds, and jumping vast distances whether horizontal or vertical. The Book of Jasher reads as if it was taken from an action-packed movie fantasy or animated cartoon adventure. When we consider people such as Johnny Chang who, being a master of his own energy, could fuse the positive and negative energies within himself and could heal people with the power of thought, we also learn that he could set things on fire with nothing but concentration on his own energy.

We can now understand how Aliyahu summoned the fire of YHWH during his confrontation with Akazyah the King of Shomeron.

AND ALIYAHU ANSWERED AND SAID TO THE CAPTAIN OF 50, "AND IF I AM A MAN OF ALAHIM, LET FIRE COME DOWN FROM THE HEAVENS AND CONSUME YOU AND YOUR FIFTY MEN." AND FIRE CAME DOWN AND CONSUMED HIM AND HIS 50. (2 Kings 1:10)

Imagination, visions and dreams are all words synonymous with sight. Imagination is extremely important in meditation, for it is the imagination of what we desire that begins the process of manifestation through the four worlds:

"The four worlds are as follows: the Atzilutic World of Existence and Emanation, the Briah World of Creation, the Yitzirah World of Formation, and the Asiyah World of Action and Manifestation." (Melchizedek Y. Lewis)

Meditation also involves imaging whether in purposeful conscious triggering or in the dreams of the night.

WHEN I REMEMBER YOU ON MY BED, I MEDITATE ON YOU IN THE NIGHT WATCHES. (Psalms 63:6)

In Asian culture the art of Chi is often referred to as meditation in movement (Tai Chi) as opposed to most examples of sitting cross legged with eyes closed. To move around in a constant state of meditation is in accordance with Hebrew scripture.

CONTENTED IS THE MAN WHO SHALL NOT WALK IN THE COUNSEL OF THE WRONG, AND SHALL NOT STAND IN THE PATH OF SINNERS, AND SHALL NOT SIT IN THE SEAT OF SCOFFERS. BUT HIS DELIGHT IS IN THE TORAH OF YHWH, AND HE "MEDITATES" IN HIS TORAH DAY AND NIGHT. (Psalms 1:2)

Yes, we can meditate on YHWH's laws day and night. This is indeed an example of Tai Chi practice present in scripture. We can heal ourselves and others with constant meditation and concentration on YHWH's laws and live for extreme periods of time.

AND NOAH LIVED AFTER THE FLOOD 350 YEARS. SO, ALL THE DAYS OF NOAH WERE 950 YEARS, AND HE DIED. (Genesis 9:28 to 29)

My son, do not forget my Torah, and let your heart mind watch over my commands, for length of days and long life they add to you. (Proverbs 3:1 to 2)

However, we must be diligent and unwavering in our faith confidence which is an action word. All of the knowledge in the world is useless without practice. The practice of the positive aspects of the universal laws of creation is the key. The fusion of the two opposites is the answer. Some people are blessed with gifts given by YHWH, others are not. Some have the gift of strength, others have the gift of healing, and the anointed ones have combinations of many divine attributes. To pray for something is to call out, ask for, be vociferous. Concentration and imagination are included as well.

MY EYES HAVE GONE BEFORE THE NIGHT WATCHES TO STUDY YOUR WORD. (Psalms 119:148)

GIVE EAR TO MY WORDS YHWH, CONSIDER MY "MEDITATION". ATTEND TO THE VOICE OF MY CRY, MY SOVEREIGN AND MY POWER, FOR TO YOU I PRAY. (Psalms 5:1 to 2)

The culture of Asian people happens to be one of, if not the most important part of our culture as Hebrews. Though the culture was lost, it has been preserved by the Eastern Asiatic culture. Now that we have some understanding of how important meditation is to the Hebrew way of life, it would be wise to study the art of Tai Chi and other forms of meditation. One must be careful to be wise and know that the word YHWH, with the understanding of its capabilities, is the most powerful word to use in meditation for the desired result of the petitioner. The pagan aspects of deity such as the elephant headed son of Shiva must not be worshipped as actual Gods.

I REJOICE AND EXULT IN YOU. I SING PRAISES TO YOUR NAME ELYON MOST HIGH. (Psalms 9:2)

These are the names our forefathers used whether in times of distress or thanksgiving and adoration.

AND I APPEARED TO ABRAHAM, TO ISSAC, AND TO JACOB AS AL SHADDAI. AND BY MY NAME YHWH WAS I NOT KNOWN TO THEM. (Exodus 6:3)

We see from the scriptures the results of their petitions.

Then Yahoshua spoke to YHWH in the day when YHWH gave the Ammorites over to the children of Israel, and he said before the eyes of Israel,

"SUN STAND STILL OVER GIBON, AND MOON IN THE VALLEY OF AYALON."

So, the sun stood still and the moon stopped till the nation avenged itself upon their enemies. Is this not written in the Book of Yashar. Thus, the sun stopped in the midst of the heavens and did not hasten to go down for an entire day. AND THERE HAS BEEN NO DAY LIKE THAT, BEFORE IT OR AFTER IT, THAT YHWH LISTENED TO THE VOICE OF A MAN, BECAUSE YHWH FOUGHT FOR ISRAEL. (Yahoshua 10:12 to 14)

So, we as a people should follow the blueprint of prayer and invocation if we desire similar results. We ought to use the same names when calling upon the Highest YHWH. Abraham, Issac and Jacob all prayed this way as well, by singing, crying out, praising, meditating with their faces to the ground in prostration and causing their hands to be spread out towards the heavens.

THE WATERS WERE SPLIT, THE SUN STOOD STILL, FIRE CAME DOWN FROM THE HEAVENS, THE LAND WAS OPENED, THE SICK WERE HEALED, ENTIRE ARMIES WERE DEFEATED, AND THE PHYSICAL DEAD WERE RAISED BACK TO LIFE. HALLELU YAH!

CHAPTER 10

Mind Of Moses

Moses, representative and leader of the Israelites, was chosen to lead the people out of Egypt and into the promised land. He pioneered the proclamation of a nation of people with the help of the power that chose him to lead. The story of Moses is critical in understanding the Mind. It is within the story of Moses that, with true understanding of the context of the narrative, we realize the power that lies within the people themselves is the same power that set them free. The cries of the people had come up to YHWH and as a result that power sent to them a savior in the person of Moses.

Imagine a small nation of people in captivity, subject to hard labors. What are the thoughts of such a people? What are their feelings and attitudes? You can be sure that they would think and say to themselves, "Oh boy, do I wish we were free," or "I cannot wait till this is over," "Somebody please help us." Eventually the creative forces will produce the desired results.

At the time of the vision of the burning bush, Moses was instructed to lead the people out of bondage and into the promised land. Moses, being doubtful, asked why the people would follow him and who he should say had sent him. Thus, the answer was AHYEH ASHAR AHYEH (I AM THAT WHICH I AM). YHWH told Moses that the cries of the children had come up to Him.

YHWH THEN SAID I HAVE SEEN THE MISERY OF MY PEOPLE IN EGYPT. I HAVE HEARD THEM CRYING FOR HELP ON ACCOUNT OF THEIR TASKMASTERS. YES, I AM AWARE OF THEIR SUFFERINGS. (Ex. 3:7)

The thoughts of the people as a collective were strong enough to will themselves into freedom. The signs and wonders that Moses performed supported the beliefs of the people for positive results. When the people began to be doubtful,

AND THE WHOLE COMMUNITY BEGAN COMPLAINING ABOUT MOSES AND AARON IN THE DESERT AND SAID UNTO THEM, "WHY DID WE NOT DIE AT THE HAND OF YHWH IN EGYPT WHERE WE USED TO SIT AROUND THE POTS OF FLESH AND COULD EAT TO OUR HEARTS DESIRE. YOU HAVE LED US INTO THIS DESERT TO STARVE THIS ENTIRE ASSEMBLY TO DEATH." (Ex. 16:2,3)

A miracle was performed to reinvigorate the positive thoughts.

YHWH SAID TO MOSES, "LOOK, I SHALL RAIN DOWN BREAD FOR YOU FROM THE HEAVENS." (Ex. 16:4)

That evening quails flew in and covered the camp and the next morning there was a layer of dew all around the camp. (Ex. 16:13)

THE WHOLE COMMUNITY OF ISRAELITES LEFT THE DESERT OF SIN, TRAVELING BY THE STAGES THAT YHWH HAD ORDERED. THEY PITCHED CAMP AT REPHAIM WHERE THERE WAS NO WATER TO DRINK. THE PEOPLE TOOK ISSUE WITH MOSES FOR THIS AND SAID, "GIVE US WATER TO DRINK." MOSES REPLIED, "WHY DO YOU TAKE ISSUE WITH ME. WHY DO YOU PUT YHWH TO THE TEST." BUT TORMENTED BY THIRST, THE PEOPLE COMPLAINED TO MOSES, "WHY DID YOU BRING US OUT OF EGYPT," THEY SAID, "ONLY TO MAKE US, OUR CHILDREN, AND OUR LIVESTOCK DIE OF THIRST." (Ex. 17:2,3)

"STRIKE THE ROCK AND WATER WILL COME OUT FOR THE PEOPLE TO DRINK." THIS IS WHAT MOSES DID, WITH THE ELDERS LOOKING ON. (Ex. 17:6)

The miracle of the Mind is produced every day. Think about how you can think of a song you have not heard in years and all of a sudden it gets played on the radio; the same station you listen to on your way to work. They never play that song until you think of it first. Or think about how you can think of a song in your own thoughts and as you stand in line at that restaurant or doctor's office, a complete stranger chimes in verbally at the exact same point in the song as you are thinking of it.

How about when we look for the love of our lives only to find disappointment time after time, and as soon as we give up and say to ourselves, "It will never happen," the person of our dreams walks right through the door. It happens this way because our Mind does not compute impossibilities. Anything the Mind can fathom to exist has the capability of being. If the manifestation were not possible, the Mind could not fathom it.

In Exodus 3:14,15 Moses told the people in so many words that the power YHWH that lies within them is what caused him to lead them to freedom, and furthermore that the power of creation and manifestation which their forefathers worshiped had sent him. Moses invigorated the Minds of the people and caused them to believe in themselves. However, belief without cooperation with Moses's instruction is useless and so belief and action go hand in hand. If you would like to have a career in the medical field, it is not likely to happen unless you study the criteria needed in order to perform your craft effectively and then submit a resume or application to the facility or company of your liking.

Just as the children of Israel made the journey to the land of Canaan, they were not magically whisked away to suddenly appear in Canaan. Also, when Pharaoh had his magicians perform the same miracles as Moses, it was an attempt at discouraging the people from performing the action of making the journey, which placed doubt in the Minds of the people.

When you submit that application to the company you want to work for and they turn you away because the position is already filled, they do not hire felons, or there is racial discrimination, it is an attempt at discouragement. But we must persevere just as Moses did for the Israelites, and miracles can occur that will make your petition undeniable.

(Prayer, meditation, thought construction, application, and perseverance are the keys in the succession of success.) With the correct understanding of the name YHWH, we can now see the Exodus story in a new light. The power that exists within the people themselves, the strength of their own belief, and the proper application and perseverance demonstrated within the pages of the Book of Exodus is an example of the power of the Mind.

The Book of Proverbs is filled with wisdom, knowledge, and guidance to deal with the situations of life. However, what does Proverbs have to do with the power of the Mind? In

Hebrew, the heart is the Mind, so when reading scripture replace the word heart with Mind and the understanding of those specific scripture verses becomes visible where there was at first unsurety.

MY CHILD, IF YOU TAKE MY WORDS TO HEART (MIND), IF YOU SET YOUR WAYS BY MY COMMANDMENTS, TURNING YOUR EAR TO WISDOM, TURNING YOUR HEART (MIND) TO UNDERSTANDING, IF YOU LOOK FOR IT AS YOU DO FOR SILVER, SEARCH FOR IT AS THOUGH FOR BURIED TREASURE, THEN YOU WILL UNDERSTAND WHAT THE REVERENCE OF YHWH IS AND DISCOVER THE KNOWLEDGE OF POWER. FOR YHWH IS THE GIVER OF WISDOM, FROM HIS MOUTH ISSUE KNOWLEDGE AND UNDERSTANDING.

(Prov. 2:1 to 6)

THE REVERENCE OF YHWH, THE UNIVERSAL POWER OF CREATION, MIND, THOUGHT, WILL TO BE AND MANIFESTATION, IS THE BEGINNING OF KNOWLEDGE. FOOLS SPURN WISDOM AND DISCIPLINE. (Prov. 1:7)

In the Hebrew language the words which define the Mind of man are indeed translated as hearts, keeping in mind that by today's standards the heart is regarded as the organ that occupies the chest area of the body and the brain is in the skull area. And so, you have a separation of these two bodily organs. Incorrect translations direct the reader of scripture to believe that we should rely on our emotions as opposed to our Minds and intellect when it comes to making sound decisions. The words that represent the Mind have either been erroneously or purposefully translated over a thousand times as heart. Just to add more weight to this truth being revealed, the heart and the brain are physical but the Mind transcends our limited physical reality. For the Mind is physical but of a different nature of which we have no understanding.

I HAVE SCRUTINIZED YHWH'S WHOLE CREATION. YOU CANNOT GET TO THE BOTTOM OF EVERYTHING TAKING PLACE UNDER THE SUN. YOU MAY WEAR YOURSELF OUT IN THE SEARCH, BUT YOU WILL NEVER FIND IT. NOT EVEN A SAGE CAN GET TO IT, EVEN IF HE SAYS THAT HE HAS DONE SO. (Eccl. 8:17)

CHAPTER 11

Mind Of Abraham

In the Book of Genesis Abraham is instructed by YHWH to leave his father's house, from the land of his father, and to begin his journey to the land of promise. However, the detail of what happened to cause Abram to follow the instructions is not given in the Book of Genesis. Like much of the sixty-six-canon version of the scriptures, many details are left out of the stories of the Biblical patriarchs. We find mostly a general synopsis of the lives of the people and the historical events. Keeping in mind that the sixty-six-canon version was compiled by foreign nations who were not of Hebrew bloodline, the sacredness of the scrolls was compromised, and the importance of other scrolls such as the Apocrypha, Pseudepigrapha, Gnostic Scriptures, and others are intentionally dismissed, which brings us to the Pseudepigrapha work of the Apocalypse of Abraham.

In the Apocalypse, Abram comes to a point in his life where he begins to question the beliefs and practices of his father Terah and his social environment. These questions came from the illogical behavior of his father in regard to the idols he worshiped. Notice in verse 1 Abram says to himself that his Heart, Mind, was distracted. *"Disturbed in my Heart Thoughts, what is this inequality that my father is doing."* (Apocalypse of Abraham 3:1 to 4)

As you can see, Abram began to use the common sense that YHWH gave him to contemplate his father's behavior. As the chapters go on Abram wants to prove to himself and to his father that the idols are worthless and have no power by his burning of the idol of Barisat and throwing other smashed idols into the river Gur, to which effect they could not save themselves. Abram understood, but his father's Mind, Heart, was hardened, stubborn.

As a result, Abram concentrated his thoughts on truth and the logic of the situation at hand and tapped into a level of consciousness that moved the creator of all things to speak to him and send him messengers, angels, to befriend him and convey to him a message to leave his father's house.

YHWH SAID TO ABRAM, LEAVE YOUR COUNTRY, YOUR KINDRED AND YOUR FATHERS HOUSE FOR A COUNTRY I WILL SHOW YOU. AND I SHALL MAKE YOU A GREAT NATION. I SHALL BLESS YOU AND MAKE YOUR NAME GREAT. YOU ARE TO BE A BLESSING. (Genesis 12:1,2)

AND IT CAME TO BE AS I WAS THINKING THINGS LIKE THESE WITH REGARD TO MY FATHER TERAH IN THE COURT OF MY HOUSE, THE VOICE OF THE MIGHTY ONE CAME DOWN FROM THE HEAVENS IN A STREAM OF FIRES SAYING AND CALLING, "ABRAM, ABRAM." AND I SAID, "HERE I AM." AND HE SAID, "YOU ARE SEARCHING FOR THE POWER OF POWERS, THE CREATOR, IN THE UNDERSTANDING OF YOUR HEART, MIND. I AM HE. GO OUT FROM TERAH YOUR FATHER AND GO OUT OF THE HOUSE THAT YOU TOO MAY NOT BE SLAIN IN THE SINS OF YOUR FATHERS HOUSE." (Apocalypse of Abraham 8:1 to 4)

I AM SENT TO YOU NOW TO BLESS YOU AND THE LAND WHICH HE WHOM YOU HAVE CALLED THE ETERNAL ONE HAS PREPARED FOR YOU. FOR YOUR SAKE I HAVE INDICATED THE WAY OF THE LAND.

(Apocalypse of Abraham 10:13,14)

Abraham's boldness and courage moved him to question even his own father's way of life. Abraham was a free thinker and could not be brainwashed into a religiously enslaved mindset.

CHAPTER 12

Teachings of Yahoshua

The New Testament writings are a collection of letters and messages that focus on the coming and purpose of a king who would save the Israelites from their woes.

SHE WILL GIVE BIRTH TO A SON AND YOU MUST NAME HIM YAHOSHUA, BECAUSE HE IS THE ONE WHO IS TO SAVE HIS PEOPLE FROM THEIR SINS. (Matt. 1:21)

AND YOU, BETHLEHEM, IN THE LAND OF YEHUDAH, YOU ARE BY NO MEANS THE LEAST AMONG YOUR LEADERS OF ISRAEL, FOR FROM YOU WILL COME A LEADER WHO WILL SHEPHERD MY PEOPLE ISRAEL. (Matt. 2:6)

Beginning with the Gospels Matthew, Mark, Luke and John the authors give detail of events from the life of the brother Yahoshua Ha Mashiack. What did the Messiah teach to his followers? He taught them how to believe or have trust in the power that lies within themselves and others. He taught them that faith is required to perform miracles and healings. Unwavering trust in the power of YHWH is essential to the entire message. For example, in the book of Matthew the Messiah is in the midst of teaching his disciples. Yahoshua gives them an assignment to carry out. However, when the father of the epileptic man gained no results from the disciples he went to Yahoshua.

MASTER, HE SAID, TAKE PITY ON MY SON. HE IS DEMENTED AND IN A WRETCHED STATE. HE IS ALWAYS FALLING INTO THE FIRE AND INTO THE WATER. I TOOK HIM TO YOUR DISCIPLES AND THEY WERE UNABLE TO CURE HIM. IN REPLY YAHOSHUA SAID, FAITHLESS AND PERVERSE GENERATION. HOW MUCH LONGER WILL I BE WITH YOU. HOW MUCH LONGER MUST I PUT UP WITH YOU. BRING HIM HERE TO ME. AND WHEN YAHOSHUA REBUKED IT THE DEVIL CAME OUT OF THE BOY, WHO WAS CURED FROM THAT MOMENT.

THEN THE DISCIPLES CAME TO HIM PRIVATELY. WHY ARE WE NOT ABLE TO DRIVE IT OUT, THEY ASKED. HE ANSWERED, BECAUSE YOU HAVE SO LITTLE FAITH. IN TRUTH, I TELL YOU IF YOU HAVE FAITH THE SIZE OF A MUSTARD SEED YOU WILL SAY TO THIS MOUNTAIN MOVE AND IT WILL BE REMOVED FROM HERE TO THERE. NOTHING WILL BE IMPOSSIBLE FOR YOU. (Matthew 17:19, 20)

Accordingly, so, Yahoshua's answer was about lack of faith which is confidence and trust. The Law of Attraction is taught and explained by Yahoshua from a non-biased point of view or perspective. However, Yahoshua does teach his students to use the Law in a positive way.

ASK AND IT WILL BE GIVEN YOU. SEARCH AND YOU WILL FIND. KNOCK AND THE DOOR WILL BE OPENED TO YOU. EVERYONE WHO ASKS RECEIVES. EVERYONE WHO SEARCHES FINDS. EVERYONE WHO KNOCKS WILL HAVE THE DOOR OPENED. IS THERE ANYONE AMONG YOU WHO WOULD HAND HIS SON A STONE WHEN HE ASKS FOR BREAD. OR WOULD HAND HIM A SNAKE WHEN HE ASKED FOR A FISH. IF YOU THEN, EVIL AS YOU ARE, KNOW HOW TO GIVE YOUR CHILDREN WHAT IS GOOD, HOW MUCH MORE WILL YOUR FATHER IN HEAVEN GIVE WHAT IS GOOD TO THOSE WHO ASK HIM. SO ALWAYS TREAT OTHERS AS YOU WOULD LIKE THEM TO TREAT YOU. THAT IS THE LAW AND THE PROPHETS. (Matthew 7:7 to 12)

Yahoshua teaches unwavering faith in the Law of Attraction and the art of manifestation.

AND AT ONCE HE MADE THE DISCIPLES GET INTO THE BOAT AND GO ON AHEAD TO THE OTHER SIDE WHILE HE SENT THE CROWDS AWAY. IN THE FOURTH WATCH OF THE NIGHT, HE CAME TOWARDS THEM WALKING ON THE SEA, AND WHEN THE DISCIPLES SAW HIM WALKING ON THE SEA, THEY WERE TERRIFIED. IT IS A GHOST, THEY SAID AND CRIED OUT IN FEAR. BUT AT ONCE YAHOSHUA CALLED OUT TO THEM SAYING, HAVE COURAGE. IT IS ME. DO NOT BE AFRAID. IT WAS PETER WHO ANSWERED. MASTER IF IT IS YOU, TELL ME TO COME AND I WILL COME TO YOU ACROSS THE WATER. YAHOSHUA SAID COME. THEN PETER GOT OUT OF THE BOAT AND STARTED WALKING ACROSS THE WATER TOWARD YAHOSHUA, BUT THEN NOTICING THE WIND HE BECAME AFRAID AND BEGAN TO SINK.

MASTER, HE CRIED, SAVE ME. YAHOSHUA PUT HIS HAND OUT AT ONCE AND HELD HIM. YOU HAVE LITTLE CONFIDENCE, HE SAID, WHY DO YOU DOUBT. AND AS THEY GOT INTO THE BOAT THE WIND DROPPED. (Matthew 14:22 to 32)

SHE HAD HEARD ABOUT YAHOSHUA AND SHE CAME UP THROUGH THE CROWD AND SHE TOUCHED HIS GARMENT FROM BEHIND THINKING, IF I CAN JUST TOUCH HIS GARMENT I SHALL BE SAVED. AND AT ONCE THE SOURCE OF THE BLEEDING DRIED UP AND SHE FELT WITHIN HERSELF THAT SHE WAS HEALED OF HER COMPLAINT. AND AT ONCE AWARE OF THE POWER THAT HAD GONE OUT FROM HIM, YAHOSHUA TURNED AROUND IN THE CROWD AND SAID, WHO TOUCHED MY GARMENT. HIS DISCIPLES SAID TO HIM, YOU SEE THE CROWD IS PRESSING AROUND YOU. HOW CAN YOU SAY WHO TOUCHED ME. BUT HE CONTINUED TO LOOK AROUND TO SEE WHO HAD DONE IT. THEN THE WOMAN CAME FORWARD FRIGHTENED AND TREMBLING BECAUSE SHE KNEW WHAT SHE HAD DONE AND WHAT HAD HAPPENED TO HER, AND SHE FELL AT HIS FEET AND TOLD HIM THE TRUTH. MY DAUGHTER, HE SAID, YOUR FAITH HAS HEALED YOU AND RESTORED YOUR HEALTH. GO IN PEACE AND BE FREE OF YOUR COMPLAINT.

The Hebrew Messiah taught his students well and just as he prophesied, they utilized the power of the Ruach ha Quodesh which is the Holy Spirit to perform miracles.

AND HE SAID TO THEM AGAIN, PEACE BE WITH YOU. AS THE FATHER SENT ME, I AM SENDING YOU. AFTER SAYING THIS HE BREATHED OUT THE HOLY SPIRIT. (John 20:21, 22)

AND HE SAID TO THEM, GO OUT TO THE WORLD. PROCLAIM THE WORD TO ALL CREATION. WHOEVER BELIEVES AND IS EMERSED WILL BE SAVED. WHOEVER DOES NOT HAVE FAITH WILL BE CONDEMNED. THESE ARE THE SIGNS THAT WILL BE ASSOCIATED WITH BELIEVERS. IN MY NAME THEY WILL CAST OUT DEMONS. THEY WILL HAVE THE GIFT OF TONGUES. THEY WILL PICK UP SNAKES IN THEIR HANDS AND BE UNHARMED SHOULD THEY DRINK DEADLY POISON. THEY WILL LAY THEIR HANDS ON THE SICK AND THEY WILL RECOVER. (Mark 16:15 to 18)

THERE HE FOUND A PARALYTIC WHO WAS CALLED AENEAS WHO HAD BEEN BEDRIDDEN FOR EIGHT YEARS. PETER SAID TO HIM, AENEAS, YAHOSHUA THE MESSIAH CURES YOU. GET UP AND MAKE YOUR BED. AENEAS GOT UP IMMEDIATELY. EVERYBODY

WHO LIVED IN LYDDA AND SHARON SAW HIM AND THEY WERE CONVERTED TO YHWH. (Acts 9:33 to 35)

PETER SENT EVERYONE OUT OF THE ROOM AND KNELT DOWN AND PRAYED. THEN HE TURNED TO THE DEAD WOMAN AND SAID, TABITHA, STAND UP. SHE OPENED HER EYES, LOOKED AT PETER AND SAT UP. PETER HELPED HER TO HER FEET. THEN HE CALLED IN THE MEMBERS OF THE CONGREGATION AND WIDOWS AND SHOWED THEM SHE WAS ALIVE. (Acts 9:40 to 42)

The power of the subconscious mind provides the ability to achieve feats thought impossible to the average person. Therefore, the knowledge of how to use the power is very rare and was only revealed to the very elect.

THEN THE DISCIPLES WENT UP TO HIM AND ASKED, WHY DO YOU SPEAK TO THEM IN PARABLES. IN ANSWER HE SAID TO THEM, BECAUSE TO YOU IS GRANTED THE MYSTERIES OF THE KINGDOM OF HEAVEN BUT TO THEM IT IS NOT GRANTED. (Matt. 13:10, 11)

Though any man who believes may experience the power, not all are allowed the knowledge of how to use and harness it. To experience the power and to know how to use it are two levels of understanding. Yahoshua belonged to the Essene Nazarites.

KNOWING ALL THAT WAS TO HAPPEN TO HIM, YAHOSHUA SAID AS HE CAME FORWARD, WHO ARE YOU LOOKING FOR. THEY ANSWERED, YAHOSHUA THE NAZARITE. HE SAID, I AM HE. (John 18:4, 5)

The Essene Nazarite sect was more than a rumor. It was fact as supported by the discovery of the Dead Sea Scrolls which unveiled the manuscripts of the Qumran Community who were undoubtedly Essenes. According to the New Testament writings Yahoshua the Hebrew Messiah was a member of the Nazir group along with John the Baptist.

BUT THE ANGEL SAID TO HIM, ZECHARIAH DO NOT BE AT ALL AFRAID, FOR YOUR PRAYER HAS BEEN HEARD. YOUR WIFE ELIZABETH IS TO BEAR YOU A SON AND YOU SHALL NAME HIM JOHN. HE WILL BE YOUR JOY AND DELIGHT AND MANY WILL REJOICE AT HIS BIRTH FOR HE WILL BE GREAT IN THE SIGHT OF YHWH. HE MUST DRINK NO WINE, NO

STRONG DRINK. EVEN FROM HIS MOTHERS WOMB HE WILL BE FILLED WITH THE SET APART SPIRIT AND HE WILL BRING BACK MANY OF THE ISRAELITES TO YHWH ALAHIM. (Matthew 1:13 to 16)

THE ANGEL OF YHWH APPEARED TO THIS WOMAN AND SAID TO HER, YOU ARE BARREN AND HAVE NO CHILD, BUT YOU ARE GOING TO CONCEIVE AND GIVE BIRTH TO A SON. FROM NOW ON TAKE GREAT CARE. DRINK NO STRONG DRINKS, WINE OR LIQUOR FERMENTED, AND EAT NO UNCLEAN THING. FOR YOU ARE GOING TO GIVE BIRTH TO A SON. NO RAZOR IS TO TOUCH HIS HEAD FOR THE BOY IS TO BE YHWH'S NAZARITE FROM HIS MOTHERS WOMB AND HE WILL SAVE ISRAEL FROM THE POWER OF THE PHILISTINES. (Judges 13:3 to 5)

PILATE WROTE OUT A NOTICE AND HAD IT FIXED TO THE TREE. IT SAID: THIS IS YAHOSHUA THE NAZARITE KING OF THE YEHUDI. (John 19:19).

YAHOSHUA Ha MASHIACK was born into a social system of corruption in regard to the laws of YHWH dealing with the Saducees and Pharisees who were in power and not so keen on practicing what they preached.

THEN YAHOSHUA SAID TO THE STUDENTS, SAYING, THE SCRIBES AND PHARISEES SIT ON THE SEAT OF MOSES. THEREFORE, WHATEVER THEY SAY TO YOU TO DO YOU SHALL DO, BUT DO NOT DO ACCORDING TO THEIR WORKS, FOR THEY SAY AND DO NOT DO. (Matt. 23:1 to 3)

Being appalled at the state of the people and the lawlessness amongst his kinsmen, he set out on a mission to teach his people to not only be hearers of the Law but to do them as well. Yahoshua was the perfect example of the Law in his time. Being a prophet like unto Moses, he was and still is a mediator between YAH and Israel just as Moses was. Yahoshua, being the focal point of the Hebrew Scriptures, set man on a course to the salvation of YAH. Many people believe that the Mashiack died for the sins of the people and that the Laws are done away with, nailed to the stake and died along with the Messiah.

People often use the writings of Paul to bolster their claims, yet they twist his teachings to their own destruction. AND RECKON THE PATIENCE OF THE MESSIAH AS

DELIVERANCE, AS ALSO OUR BELOVED BROTHER PAUL WROTE TO YOU ACCORDING TO THE WISDOM GIVEN TO HIM, AS ALSO IN ALL OF HIS OTHER LETTERS SPEAKING TO THEM CONCERNING THESE MATTERS, IN WHICH SOME ARE HARD TO UNDERSTAND, WHICH THOSE WHO ARE UNTAUGHT TWIST TO THEIR OWN DESTRUCTION AS THEY DO ALSO THE OTHER LETTERS. (2 Peter 3:15 to 16)

As in the other New Testament writings, Paul is used as the middle man between Yahoshua and the seekers of the Truth. So let us try cutting out the middle man and hear straight from the source.

DO NOT THINK THAT I CAME TO VANISH THE TORAH OR THE PROPHETS. I DID NOT COME TO DESTROY BUT TO CARRY OUT. FOR TRULY I SAY TO YOU, TILL HEAVENS AND EARTH PASS AWAY, ONE YOD OR ONE TITTLE SHALL BY NO MEANS PASS AWAY FROM THE LAW TILL ALL BE DONE. WHOEVER BREAKS ONE OF THESE COMMANDS AND TEACHES MAN SO SHALL BE LEAST IN THE KINGDOM OF THE HEAVENS, BUT WHOEVER DOES AND TEACHES THEM HE SHALL BE CALLED GREAT IN THE KINGDOM OF THE HEAVENS. (Matt. 5:17 to 19)

I HAVE CALLED HEAVENS AND EARTH AS WITNESSES AGAINST YOU TODAY. I HAVE SET FOR YOU LIFE AND DEATH, THE BLESSING AND THE CURSE. THEREFORE, CHOOSE LIFE THAT YOU MAY LIVE, BOTH YOU AND YOUR SEED. (Deuteronomy 30:19)

As we can see clearly, Yahoshua came to fulfill and do the Laws and not forsake them. According to the Laws of Moses, which are really YAH'S Laws, the Messiah wore his tassels. AND YHWH SAID TO MOSES, SAYING, SPEAK TO THE CHILDREN OF ISRAEL AND YOU SHALL SAY TO THEM TO MAKE TASSELS ON THE CORNERS OF THEIR GARMENTS THROUGHOUT THEIR GENERATIONS, AND TO PUT A BLUE CORD IN THE TASSELS OF THE CORNERS. (Numbers 15:37 to 38)

MAKE TASSELS ON THE FOUR CORNERS OF THE GARMENT WITH WHICH YOU COVER YOURSELF. (Deuteronomy 22:12)

AND SEE, A WOMAN WHO HAD A FLOW OF BLOOD FOR TWELVE YEARS CAME FROM BEHIND AND TOUCHED HIS GARMENT ON THE TASSELS. FOR SHE SAID, IF I ONLY TOUCH HIS GARMENT I SHALL BE HEALED. (Matthew 9:20 to 21)

The Messiah also observed the Passover and the Feast of Unleavened Bread. AND THESE ARE THE APPOINTED TIMES OF YHWH WHICH YOU ARE TO PROCLAIM AT THEIR APPOINTED TIMES. IN THE FIRST MONTH ON THE FOURTEENTH DAY OF THE MONTH BETWEEN THE EVENINGS IS THE PASSOVER TO YHWH. AND ON THE FIFTEENTH DAY OF THIS MONTH IS THE FESTIVAL OF UNLEAVENED BREAD TO YHWH. FOR SEVEN DAYS YOU EAT UNLEAVENED BREAD. (Leviticus 23:4 to 6)

The Messiah Yahoshua also kept the Shabbat according to the word of his Father YHWH. SPEAK TO THE CHILDREN OF ISRAEL AND SAY TO THEM, THE APPOINTED TIMES OF YHWH WHICH YOU ARE TO PROCLAIM AS SET APART, MY MOEDIM ARE THESE. SIX DAYS YOU SHALL WORK, BUT THE SEVENTH IS A DAY OF REST. YOU DO NO WORK. IT IS A SHABBATH IN ALL YOUR DWELLINGS. (Leviticus 23:2)

AND THE SHABBATH HAD COME AND HE BEGAN TO TEACH IN THE ASSEMBLY. (Mark 6:2)

AND HE CAME TO NAZERETH WHERE HE HAD BEEN BROUGHT UP, AND ACCORDING TO HIS PRACTICE HE WENT INTO THE CONGREGATION ON THE SHABBATH DAY AND STOOD UP TO READ. (Luke 4:16)

Yes, that is right. Keeping the Shabbaths was his custom. And Paul, being an imitator of the Messiah, made the Shabbath observance his practice as well. AND ACCORDING TO HIS CUSTOM, PAUL WENT IN TO THEM AND FOR THREE SHABBATHS WAS REASONING WITH THEM FROM THE SCRIPTURES. (Acts 17:2)

The Messiah also acknowledged the Hanukah, which is a celebration of the Maccabean victory over the Greek Empire around the period of one hundred sixty-five B.C.E. AND AT THAT TIME THE WINTER CAME TO BE AND THE HANUKAH CAME TO BE, AND YAHOSHUA WAS WALKING IN THE SET APART PLACE IN THE PORCH OF SOLOMON. (John 10:22 to 23)

Clearly, by the practice of the Messiah, we see he followed the word of YAH to the letter. Yahoshua held the prophet Moses in the highest regard. DO NOT THINK THAT I SHALL ACCUSE YOU TO THE FATHER. THERE IS ONE WHO ACCUSES YOU, MOSES IN WHOM YOU SET YOUR EXPECTATION. FOR IF YOU BELIEVED MOSES, YOU WOULD HAVE BELIEVED ME SINCE HE WROTE ABOUT ME. BUT IF YOU DO NOT BELIEVE HIS WRITINGS HOW SHALL YOU BELIEVE MY WORDS. (John 5:45 to 47)

BUT THERE WAS A RICH MAN WHO USED TO DRESS IN PURPLE AND FINE LINEN AND LIVED WELL EVERY DAY. AND THERE WAS A POOR BEGGAR NAMED ALAZAR WHO WAS COVERED WITH SORES, WHO WAS PLACED AT HIS GATE AND LONGED TO BE FED WITH THE CRUMBS OF HIS TABLE. INDEED, EVEN THE DOGS CAME AND LICKED HIS SORES. AND IT CAME TO BE THAT THE BEGGAR DIED AND WAS CARRIED AWAY BY THE MESSENGERS TO THE BOSOM OF ABRAHAM. AND THE RICH MAN ALSO DIED AND WAS BURIED. AND WHILE SUFFERING THE TORTURES IN SHEOL, HAVING LIFTED UP HIS EYES, HE SAW ABRAHAM FAR OFF AND ALAZAR IN HIS BOSOM. AND HE CRIED OUT AND SAID, FATHER ABRAHAM, HAVE KINDNESS ON ME AND SEND ALAZAR TO DIP THE TIP OF HIS FINGER INTO THE WATER AND COOL MY TONGUE, FOR I AM SUFFERING IN THIS FLAME. BUT ABRAHAM SAID, SON, REMEMBER THAT IN YOUR LIFE YOU RECEIVED YOUR BLESSINGS AND LIKEWISE ALAZAR THE EVIL. BUT NOW HE IS COMFORTED AND YOU ARE SUFFERING. AND BESIDES ALL THIS, BETWEEN YOU AND US A BARRIER HAS BEEN SET SO THAT THOSE WHO WISH TO PASS FROM HERE TO THERE ARE UNABLE, NOR DO THOSE FROM THERE PASS TO US. AND HE SAID, THEN I BEG YOU FATHER THAT YOU WOULD SEND HIM TO MY FATHERS HOUSE, FOR I HAVE FIVE BROTHERS. LET HIM WARN THEM LEST THEY ALSO COME TO THIS PLACE OF THE TORTURES. ABRAHAM SAID TO HIM, THEY HAVE MOSES AND THE PROPHETS, LET THEM HEAR THEM. AND HE SAID, NO FATHER ABRAHAM, BUT IF SOMEONE FROM THE DEAD GOES TO THEM, THEY SHALL REPENT. BUT HE SAID TO HIM, IF THEY DO NOT HEAR MOSES AND THE PROPHETS, NEITHER WOULD THEY BE PERSUADED EVEN IF ONE SHOULD ARISE FROM THE DEAD. (Luke 16:19 to 31)

Yahoshua explains how all of YAH's laws hang on the balance of the two commands. He does this because if you really think about it, if you love your neighbor as you love yourself then you would not steal from them, you would not hurt them in any way, you would not lust after his or her spouse and you would be there for the person in their time of need. You would honor any promises or oaths between you and your friend as you would expect them to do the same for you. Therefore, all of YAH's laws surely fall under these two, to listen to Yah, love YHWH and observe the universal laws of YAH which advocate for the right and just ways of society.

AND ONE OF THEM DID QUESTION HIM SAYING, TEACHER WHAT IS THE GREATEST COMMAND IN THE TORAH AND YAHOSHUA SAID TO HIM, YOU SHALL LOVE YOUR ELOHIM WITH ALL YOUR HEART AND WITH ALL YOUR MIGHT AND WITH ALL YOUR BEING. THIS IS THE GREAT COMMAND. AND THE SECOND IS LIKE IT, YOU SHALL LOVE YOUR NEIGHBOR AS YOURSELF. ON THESE TWO HANG ALL THE TORAH AND THE PROPHETS. (Matt. 22:35 to 40)

When posed the question, good teacher what shall I do to have everlasting life, the response was, AND HE SAID TO THEM, WHY DO YOU CALL ME GOOD. NO ONE IS GOOD EXCEPT ONE, YHWH. BUT IF YOU WISH TO ENTER INTO EVERLASTING LIFE KEEP THE COMMANDS. (Matt. 19:17) And those going forth and those who followed cried out saying, hoshia na blessed is he who is coming in the name of YHWH.

There is a misconception of the wording of the sacred scriptures because our misunderstanding has been given to us by gentile nations. The New Testament was comprised of the Gospels and letters of the Apostle Paul who was raised under Roman gentile influence. As the sixty six canon version of the scriptures was selected by Emperor Constantine, King James and other gentiles over the years, being translated by those who did not have a proper understanding of scripture, and those who did have a true understanding hid the truth purposely to cause confusion amongst the people of Israel so they would not know how to worship YHWH in the correct way, all the while keeping a firm grip on the positions of power over the nations of the world.

One of the best tools for gaining understanding is the method of comparative study, so let us examine some of the sayings of the Mashiak and some other scripture verses in the Bible and Gospels. When Yahoshua spoke, he spoke with scripture, the Old Testament. He did this quite often. For example, when Yahoshua was tempted by the adversary in Matthew 4:1 to 10 the Messiah fought back by quoting scripture.

BUT HE ANSWERED AND SAID, IT HAS BEEN WRITTEN MAN SHALL NOT LIVE BY BREAD ALONE BUT BY EVERY WORD THAT COMES FROM THE MOUTH OF YHWH. This verse originates in Deuteronomy chapter 8 verse 3. Satan then tried to fight the Mashiak with scripture as well. AND HE SAID TO HIM, IF YOU ARE THE SON OF ELOHIM THROW YOURSELF DOWN FOR IT WAS WRITTEN, HE SHALL COMMAND HIS MESSENGERS CONCERNING YOU AND, IN THEIR HANDS, THEY SHALL BEAR YOU UP SO THAT YOU DO NOT DASH YOUR FOOT AGAINST A STONE.

However, the Mashiak was persistent.

YAHOSHUA SAID TO HIM, IT HAS ALSO BEEN WRITTEN, YOU SHALL NOT TRY OR TEST YHWH YOUR ELOHIM. AGAIN, THE DEVIL TOOK HIM UP ON A VERY HIGH MOUNTAIN AND SHOWED HIM ALL THE KINGDOMS OF THE EARTH AND SAID TO HIM, ALL THESE I GIVE TO YOU IF YOU FALL DOWN AND WORSHIP ME. THEN YAHOSHUA SAID TO HIM, GO SHATAN, FOR IT HAS BEEN WRITTEN YOU SHALL WORSHIP YHWH YOUR ELOHIM AND HIM ALONE SHALL YOU SERVE. (Matt. 4:7 to 10)

When John the Baptist was locked away in prison he heard about the works of Yahoshua and he sent two of his taught ones to investigate the matters. When John's students questioned the Mashiak he answered with scripture.

GO REPORT TO JOHN WHAT YOU SEE AND HEAR. BLIND RECEIVE SIGHT AND LAME WALK, LEPERS ARE CLEANSED AND DEAF HEAR, THE DEAD ARE RAISED UP AND POOR ARE BROUGHT THE MESSAGE. AND BLESSED IS HE WHO DOES NOT STUMBLE IN ME. (Matt. 11:4 to 6)

THEN THE EYES OF THE BLIND SHALL BE OPENED AND THE EARS OF THE DEAF SHALL BE OPENED AND THE LAME SHALL LEAP LIKE A DEER AND THE TONGUE OF THE DUMB SHALL SING BECAUSE WATER SHALL BURST FORTH IN THE WILDERNESS AND STREAMS IN THE DESERT. (Isaiah 35:5 to 6)

THE SPIRIT OF THE MASTER YHWH IS UPON ME BECAUSE YHWH HAS INDEED ANOINTED ME TO BRING THE MESSAGE TO THE POOR. (Isaiah 61:1)

Now the writer of Matthew again uses Hebrew scripture in chapter 12:18 to 21. SEE MY BELOVED SERVANT WHOM I HAVE CHOSEN, MY BELOVED IN WHOM MY BEING DELIGHTS. I SHALL PUT MY SPIRIT UPON HIM AND HE SHALL DECLARE RIGHT RULING TO THE NATIONS. HE SHALL NOT STRIVE NOR CRY OUT NOR SHALL ANYONE HEAR HIS VOICE IN THE STREETS. A CRUSHED REED HE SHALL NOT BREAK AND A SMOKING FLAX HE SHALL NOT QUENCH TILL HE BRINGS FORTH RIGHT RULING FOREVER. AND THE NATIONS SHALL TRUST IN HIS NAME.

However, when you turn to the scripture in Isaiah from which he quotes the wording turns out to be quite different.

HE DOES NOT BECOME WEAK OR CRUSHED UNTIL HE HAS ESTABLISHED RIGHT RULING IN THE EARTH AND THE COASTLANDS WAIT FOR HIS TORAH. (Isaiah 42:1 to 4)

We ask ourselves why the change in wording. As always, the answer is in the scriptures. FROM THESE THE COASTLANDS, PEOPLES OF THE NATIONS, WERE SEPARATED INTO THEIR LANDS, EVERYONE ACCORDING TO THEIR CLANS INTO THEIR NATIONS. So, you see, the coastlands are the nations, so there is not a change to the passage, it is just a different way of saying it and expressing the meaning. As with this same verse the word name is used in Matthew and the word Torah is used in Isaiah. Torah and name are synonymous with each other in much scripture. And so it is not the actual utterance of the name of the Mashiak alone that matters, it is the very action of keeping the commands.

Although the utter of sound is important, we as human beings are inhabitants of a physical reality and we believe naturally that we must use that which is physical as we do know it, to attract what is not readily seen or yet felt. Therefore, we call out with the tool of belief until we can attract that which we seek.

In Buddhist meditation a person would produce the sound vibration Oooommmmmm until he or she builds up enough of their own spiritual energy until they experience results. In Hebrew meditation and invocation, one invokes the name of our Creator YHWH until he gets the same results as the Buddhist. Similar energy is being drawn by both petitioners however it is the foundation of the universal laws of our Creator in the heart, mind and thoughts of the person that will determine if the person is dealing with a constructive or destructive force. The universal laws of creation along with the productive laws of man are summed up in the name YHWH or simply YAH. Therefore, meditating and invoking this name along with the correct understanding and definition of the name produces energy that is conducive to gaining the knowledge of how to exist eternally.

The name Yahoshua by definition means Yah's salvation and Yah's salvation is the law and command of YHWH. So, with the understanding that the spoken words YHWH and Yahoshua are in agreement with each other, the name Yahoshua is also acceptable. However, it is not entirely necessary, it is all about the confidence and trust of the petitioner.

AND THERE IS NO DELIVERANCE IN ANYONE OR ANYTHING ELSE FOR THERE IS NO OTHER NAME OR LAW UNDER THE HEAVEN GIVEN TO MAN BY WHICH WE NEED TO BE DELIVERED. (Acts 4:12)

The above verse is speaking of Yahoshua Ha Mashiak, see Acts 12:10. However in the same book of Acts in the second chapter it says this. AND IT SHALL BE THAT EVERYONE WHO CALLS ON THE NAME OF YHWH SHALL BE DELIVERED. (Acts 2:21) The author of Acts is quoting from the prophet Yoel in chapter 2 verse 32. In the following examples we will replace the word name with laws or commands and find that we get a better understanding of scripture where there was once uncertainty.

AND NOW WHAT HAVE I HERE DECLARES YHWH THAT MY PEOPLE ARE TAKEN AWAY FOR NOTHING. THOSE THAT RULE OVER THEM MAKE THEM WAIL DECLARES YHWH AND MY COMMANDS ARE DESPISED ALL DAY CONTINUALLY. THEREFORE, MY PEOPLE SHALL KNOW MY TORAH IN THAT DAY FOR I AM THE ONE SPEAKING SEE IT IS I. (Isaiah 52:5 to 6)

FOR THUS SAYS THE HIGH AND EXALTED ONE WHO DWELLS FOREVER WHOSE TORAH IS SET APART. (Isaiah 57:15)

WE HAVE BECOME LIKE THOSE OVER WHOM YOU NEVER RULED. YOUR COMMANDMENTS OR NAME IS NOT KEPT AMONGST THEM. (Isaiah 63:19)

HERE I AM TO A NATION NOT CALLING ON MY NAME, NOT KEEPING MY COMMANDS. (Isaiah 65:1)

AND THIS IS HIS COMMAND THAT WE SHOULD FOLLOW THE INSTRUCTIONS OF HIS TORAH AND LOVE ONE ANOTHER AS HE GAVE US COMMAND. (First John 3:23)

And Peter said to them, repent and let each one of you be immersed in the name, Torah, for forgiveness of sins. And you shall receive the gift of the Holy Spirit, Ruach Ha Qodesh. (Acts 2:38)

He who believes in him is not judged, but he who does not believe is judged already because he has not believed in the name, commandments and Torah, of the exalted powers. (Gospel of John 3:18)

BLESSED IS HE WHO TEACHES AND LIVES BY THE TORAH. (Matt. 21:19)

The author of the Gospel of Matthew is quoting from Psalms 119:1. Keep in mind that the words name and Torah are synonymous in scripture. In Hebrew scripture poetry is dominant, the problem is that people relate rhythm with poetry according to the modern standard. The Hebrew language is naturally rhythmic and the poetry aspect comes with the beauty of expression. The more ways you can find to express or describe any person, place or thing or even an idea is poetic in Hebrew culture. The book of Psalms being a perfect example, in chapter 119 the chapter in its entirety expresses the love, respect, adoration, thanks and admiration of YHWH's laws. The writer is actually saying the same thing over again. Remember as you read that the words law, Torah, order, right ruling, commands, truth, name and witness have the exact same meaning which is the Torah and universal laws.

Another great example is the vow of the Nazarite in the book of Numbers chapter 6:23 to 27. In verse 25 it says YHWH make his face shine upon you. In verse 26 it says YHWH lift up his face upon you. Once again, the writer is using different groups of words to express the same meaning and message which is to show you favor and give you peace. The book of Psalms, Lamentations and Songs of Solomon are known for poetry however unknown to the reader close to seventy percent of scripture from Genesis to Malachi is poetic in nature. All you have to do is look for the repetition.

In the beginning was the word or law and the word or law was with YHWH and the word was YHWH. He was in the beginning with YHWH. All came to be through him, the self-existing universal laws of creation, and without them not even one that came to be came to be.

Without the laws the planet Earth would not be able to stay its course around the sun. It would fall from its place into an endless abyss of space and time. The planets in our solar system would follow suit and be thrown into a chaotic frenzy. Without the laws existence as we know it would not have existed at all. To create means to produce therefore our Creator gave the children of Israel the laws to ensure them a positive life sustaining and productive society. The flip side to all of this is balance. When the world became so negatively influenced in the days of Noah YHWH caused a flood to rid the world of evil by using the power of water for the destruction of the world's inhabitants. Ironically at the same time this event is a period of cleansing for the earth and its occupants to come.

At the time before the flood man's lifespan could have easily reached a thousand years. Imagine a world full of sin committed by people who lived such a long-time spreading negativity and destruction on earth. Something had to be done about this so YHWH caused the flood and saved Noah in whom he found to be righteous, yet YHWH shortened the life of man to one hundred twenty years by adding the consumption of flesh to his diet. AND YHWH SAID, MY SPIRIT SHALL NOT STRIVE WITH MAN FOREVER IN HIS GOING ASTRAY. HE IS FLESH AND HIS DAYS SHALL BE ONE HUNDRED TWENTY YEARS. (Genesis 6:3) EVERY MOVING CREATURE THAT LIVES IS FOOD FOR YOU AS I GAVE THE GREEN PLANTS. (Genesis 9:3)

YHWH is the creator of good and evil. Without good there could be no bad and vice versa. By keeping the good and positive laws of YHWH, it puts man in a state of uplifting behavior, good health and confidence in his position in the kingdom of YHWH. Those who are behaving in a negative way are making the free willed decision to accept the destructive aspects of creation in their lives. The goal of the scriptures is to spread the positive aspects of the universal laws of creation all throughout the earth. YHWH is the initial spark that used the word or law which is his salvation to bring all things into existence.

Yahoshua Ha Mashiak represents YHWH's laws on earth in this physical reality as we know it. Every time you adhere to YHWH's law you are in the midst of the positive aspects of the universal laws of creation and the universal laws of creation or Yahoshua are in the midst of you.

In Conclusion, all religions, from ancient Eastern to ancient Egyptian, all doctrines, allude to the power of the creative forces being pure energy and consciousness. The answer to life's mysteries is beyond any human understanding. All we can do is accept the boundaries of knowledge and apply what we do know for the embetterment of all mankind.

The Hebrew way of life has preserved for thousands of years the culture of the pre-dynastic world civilizations, to which we owe our doctrines of meditation and oneness with the All, the I AM. All things have been created in the spiritual realms and are now being played out in the physical environment. All prophecies of YHWH will come to pass and cannot be avoided. Simply put, growth is the nature of all that exists, and anything that advocates for the hindrance of production is in opposition to the creative force.

Whose side are you on?

THE BIBLIOGRAPHY

i. Apocalypse of Abraham / Pseudopigripha

ii. Mysteries of Melchizedek, Melchizedek Y. Lewis

iii. I.S.R. Translation, I.S.R. Institute

iv. King James Version (Bible Translation)

v. Hans Jenny, Cymatics, 2 vols., 1974, Basilius Press 2/p.106

vi. Merriam-Webster's Dictionary

vii. Universal Kabbalah, Lenora Leet

viii. Book of Enoch

ix. Strongs Concordance

x. J.P.S. Tanak (Scripture Translation)

xi. Anacalypsis, Godfrey S. Higgins

www.ingramcontent.com/pod-product-compliance
Lightning Source LLC
Chambersburg PA
CBHW080733020726
47503CB00010B/2901